THE WOLF CUB
OF SPARTA

THE WOLF CUB OF SPARTA

J RYAN

The Book Guild Ltd

First published in Great Britain in 2023 by
The Book Guild Ltd
Unit E2 Airfield Business Park,
Harrison Road, Market Harborough,
Leicestershire. LE16 7UL
Tel: 0116 2792299
www.bookguild.co.uk
Email: info@bookguild.co.uk
Twitter: @bookguild

This work is entirely fictitious and bears no resemblance to any persons living or dead.

Typeset in 11pt Minion Pro

Printed and bound by CPI Group (UK) Ltd, Croydon, CR0 4YY

ISBN 978 1915352 552

British Library Cataloguing in Publication Data.
A catalogue record for this book is available from the British Library.

ONE

CHARIOTS OF FIRE

Our naked feet make no sound on the stones of the mountainside. Flitting from one thin bush to another, Zena and I are shadows. Even our breathing is silent. The goddess Selene is with us tonight. From time to time, she shows her radiant face behind trailing clouds.

In the pastures a thousand feet below, the sheep too are quiet. They know better than to make a noise at night. If the amber eyes of the killer advance on them, there'll be just time to bleat one warning. Then sharp teeth will close on soft throat and it'll be over. But hopefully, not tonight. Not our sheep. After tonight, hopefully, it will be someone else's.

Zena is at my side. 'I have his scent!' She's pulled up a handful of dry grass and is rubbing it in her palm. She sniffs and passes it to me.

And there it is. The musky dirt smell. 'Can you tell which way he's going?'

'He could be in front of us; right over our heads.'

The thought chills me. Not because the wolf might attack us: he has no need with plenty of easier prey around. But because he is so much cleverer than we are. I whisper, 'So, what do we do?'

'This.' She takes the warm stillborn lamb from the bag round her shoulders and with a small knife makes a nick in a limb. Dark drops of blood fall onto the stones. 'Now, we keep going.'

We move faster as we ascend the ridge. The Grey One will be hot on our heels now, inflamed by the scent of lamb's blood. And this is what we want. Luring him away from our flocks and towards someone else's. We reach the ridge, step over the narrow spine and start the slippery descent. Something makes me glance behind. At the same moment, Selene glides out from the clouds and shines on the silver crest of a huge grey wolf on a ledge just above us. I stand still in shock. But he's not tensed to spring. He's motionless, head slightly on one side; like he's thinking.

'Lycon, come *on*!' Zena's seen the wolf but she's on her way. Slipping and sliding on the steep, scree-covered slope that will take us towards the valley. I follow, stumbling and tumbling. I don't have her balance or her strong legs. She waits for me at the bottom of the slope, shaking quietly with laughter at my clumsy antics. I arrive on my backside in a cloud of dust. She yanks me up and we dive into the cover of skinny bushes as we make the rest of the descent towards the nursery slopes.

'Here?' Zena takes the sad little corpse from the bag.

'One moment.' I take a small vial from my tunic and trickle a few drops of wine onto the body. 'At least we can dedicate it to Artemis – not just abandon…' I don't know what has made me stop. Except that the skin on the back of my neck has started to prickle. And Zena is already looking up at something behind me. I turn.

Moonlight illuminates the long pale hair of the silent, nearly naked men standing on the cliff twenty feet above us. It glints on their daggers, the only weapons they carry. And it gleams on the short, vicious sword of their helmeted and breast-plated leader as he thrusts it towards us. It's a stabbing sword, designed for close-quarters combat. Its jagged edges can slash through arteries in far less time than it takes you to draw your last breath.

Behind the eyeholes of the leader's helmet there is only darkness. His arm never moves as he points the sword towards us. The whole troop could have risen up from the clifftop like avenging ghosts: sinuous, sudden, silent. This is the Krypteia. Sparta's secret service, with the best young graduates from its elite university. Combination police force, spy network and assassin squad. Living rough, patrolling stealthily at night to protect against robber gangs, gathering intelligence and maintaining security. Crushing any hint of helot slave rebellion with instant death. I guess two teenagers with a dead lamb must look pretty threatening.

When the leader speaks, his voice is ominously quiet. 'Whose slaves are you?'

From her crouching position, Zena stands. I wonder if this is wise, but Zena doesn't kneel to anyone. More slowly, I straighten up. She says, 'We work for Milos, the sheep farmer in the next valley.' Mesmerised, I stare at the sharp tip of the sword.

'What are you doing out here at night?' He gestures with his sword at me. 'Let the girl answer!' I am only too glad to let Zena continue.

'Our sheep are being threatened by a wolf.'

'Ah… and you are setting a trap?'

'Yes, sir.' Zena's tone is polite, but she gazes unflinchingly up at the hollow eyes looking down at her.

'And how will you kill the wolf when he takes the bait? You are unarmed, aren't you?' I stiffen. Is this a cue for them to search us? If so, they'll find Zena's little knife – a treasonable offence punished by instant execution.

Zena stoops and picks up a jagged stone. 'Lycon will hold the wolf while I smash its skull in.' I try not to shudder at the horrible thought.

The leader's voice is mocking. 'Your brother is strong enough to catch and hold down a wolf while you administer the death blows?' I'm not Zena's brother but now is not the time to argue. I try to stand straight, shuffling my badly behaving leg into line.

Zena's voice is firm. 'Yes, sir. Lycon is very strong.'

The leader laughs, lowering his sword. 'Strong, are you, Lycon? Then just be thankful that we don't choose to take your wolf bait for our supper. Now get back under the roof where you belong. If we find you again, you'll be sent flying from the top of the mountain!' The troop melts into the night as silently as they came.

I look at the dead lamb. 'That's torn it. You can bet the wolf's high-tailed it back to our sheep now.'

'And I'll bet he hasn't! Let's clear out and make some space for him.'

With the certain feeling that we're being watched by many pairs of eyes, we scramble back up the ridge and make our weary way home to our flock. Zena is right. No sheep or lambs are missing and they all look happy enough. We go back into the stone shepherd's hut and take it in turns to sleep and stand guard until dawn tips the mountain with a rosy glow.

*

I'm pretty sure I'm not Zena's brother. There are just so many ways that we're nothing like each other. The only thing we have in common is that we were both plucked off Mount Taygetos by Milos and his wife in the middle of the night. I came first. The city elders didn't like my shrivelled lower leg – I'd never be any good for the army. It didn't bother Milos and Myra; and it didn't stop me learning to walk, in my own way. My arms and shoulders got very strong from always grabbing things to keep moving.

Myra told me that they rescued Zena from the mountain a few months after me. Girls get dumped more often than boys because it's fighting men they want. It's a shame because the army would do really well with Zena; she's tall and strong and incredibly fast. And she's not afraid of anything.

Milos and Myra are decent folk and they've always been good to us. Myra said they couldn't have children of their own to help look after their farm, so finding us on the mountain was like a gift from the gods. Other couples go up there too, not always as kind as Milos and Myra – so I reckon we all got lucky.

*

We might have gotten away with it that first night when we bumped into the Krypteia, but our luck began to change a month later when we were up the mountain again, looking for a lost sheep. We'd never mentioned the K word to Milos and Myra – they had enough to worry about. But on this trip, Zena decided not to take her knife, just in case they found us again and searched us this time.

A wind was blowing as we moved into autumn and it was making this keening noise around the rock formations as we went higher. Sometimes it sounded like the wolf howling. I didn't mind that, as long as he was well clear of our sheep.

Then, as we're nearing the ridge into the next valley, we see a faint glow just beyond the rocks which makes us stop dead. Zena whispers, 'What *idiots* are lighting fires?'

We creep to the top of the ridge and look down. Six men in helot tunics like us are stoking the fire with branches they've gathered from the bushes. Two of them are holding a struggling sheep. We know what they're planning. Even if that sheep hadn't been ours, we'd still have done the same thing. Like a tigress, Zena pounces from the ridge and tears the sheep from them. I follow, wrestling them back as they fight her for the prize. Zena shouts, 'It's our sheep!'

Terrified, the animal thrashes even more violently.

'It's ours now,' says a gruff voice. The burliest of the group comes between me and the men I'm trying to fight off. 'Just leave us be and you'll come to no harm.'

Zena is hanging on fiercely to the sheep and the men hesitate to try and wrest it from her. She hisses, 'It's our sheep – look at the red dye mark on its back!'

The burly man scratches his head. He turns to a comrade. 'Can you see a mark, Orrin?'

His companion looks closely at the panicking sheep. 'Funny you should say that, Nicos. Can't see any mark, me.'

Nicos says, 'So, just give the sheep back to us, there's a good girl.'

No one, in this world or the next, calls Zena a good girl. Thrusting the sheep into my arms, she lands a kick right in the centre of Nicos' chest that knocks all the air out of his lungs. He staggers, wheezing for breath. Then, before anyone can move, she grabs Orrin's and Nicos' heads and bangs them together so hard you can hear bone against bone. They slump to the ground. Breathing only slightly harder, she takes a stand against the remaining four men, legs braced, arms ready.

I see my chance and loose the sheep, shouting, 'Run, you silly bugger! Home!' It tears off up the slope on agile legs. Artemis only knows if that sheep will make it back to her flock. Two of the men start to make a run for it after the sheep, then they stop abruptly halfway up towards the ridge. I don't need to look; nor do I want to. These stupid men with their fire have done for us.

*

After the Krypteia have marched the six helots away, to what fate I can only think of with a cold dread, the leader remains behind. Holding his stabbing sword, he stands next to the dying embers of the fire, the flames striking gold reflections from his bronze breastplate. Zena and I stand side by side, waiting to be decreed a fate similar to the slaves. Nothing can save us now. We've been found in a fight with a bunch of helots who face summary execution simply for being out after dark. I feel bitterly sorry for Milos and Myra, who won't have anyone to help them anymore. Just because we weren't clever enough to keep out of trouble.

Then the leader does something that neither of us is expecting. He removes his sword belt. Then he takes off his breastplate and lays it on the ground. Finally, he lifts the helmet from his head. Flaxen hair falls around his shoulders. The eyes, no longer hooded by the helmet, are as blue as the Aegean. With astonishment, I realise that he can't be much older than I am. His voice still has the quietness of our first encounter. 'So, Wolf Eyes, your sister says you are strong.'

Zena says I have amber eyes, the same colour as a wolf. I'll take her word for it; mirrors are a luxury that Milos and Myra have no need for. I shift my joker leg and look at the muscles that ripple from his jaw to his hips. 'Probably not as strong as you.'

'Probably not, with that leg.' He stoops and picks up his sword, hefting it in his left hand. 'My right hand is my sword hand. Can you make me drop my sword from my weaker hand?'

I have to laugh. 'Before or after you've cut off my legs and everything between them?'

A flash crosses his eyes; it could be annoyance. Or is it humour? Not something you'd expect from the leader of an execution squad. 'You'll have to trust me, Wolf Eyes.'

'Then don't patronise me, Swordsman! I'll take you on with the sword in your sword hand.'

He takes the sword in his right hand. 'Do you have any conditions?'

I growl, 'Zena starts us. And she's not my sister!'

Zena immediately shouts the command and I reach straight for him – my right hand to his left arm and vice versa. My throwaway comment has done exactly what I wanted; he's just a bit taken aback. My left hand has his right wrist in a grip like a vice before he can brace it. And try as he might, he can't get the advantage. We strain together, shoulder to shoulder, breathing hard, sweat starting to run. Then I can feel my damn leg starting to go and I have to finish this quickly. Like I'm grabbing our ram and hoisting him before he can gore me, I chuck my adversary clean over my back. His arms are twisting so much that the bones will break: he has no choice but to let go the sword. I dance to one side as it just misses my toes. Then my leg goes and I fall over.

His hand grasps mine and pulls me up. 'You win, Wolf Eyes. But not because you're stronger.'

'Have to make up for it in other ways, don't I?'

Zena picks up the murderous sword and looks at it appraisingly in the dimming light of the fire. Then she hurls it high in the air, spinning and flashing until it plummets down, catching it deftly by the hilt she passes it back to its owner. 'He's smarter than you and me. He's the brains – I'm the legs.'

Lowering the blade, the leader says, 'You win your races, do you, Swordswoman?'

She tosses her slick of dark hair. 'Against girls, of course I do.'

I brush the dust off my sweaty arms. 'She's challenging you, Swordsman.'

'We don't race girls. It wouldn't be fair.'

Zena's voice is as mocking as the Swordsman's was the first time we fell into the clutches of the Krypteia. 'Wouldn't be fair on whom?'

The course is two miles, traversing the mountain to the first tall tree and back. As I start them, Zena's long legs blur through the split sides of her tunic. The leader follows at a steady lope; he's playing a waiting game. He doesn't know that to Zena a two-mile sprint is very little different to a two hundred-yard one. I won't have to wait long.

The leader's had to up his game by the time they reappear over the ridge. But it's too late for him to catch Zena. She's barely dropped any speed at all as she flashes over the finish line. She's scooping up water at the nearby stream that tumbles down the rocks, when he finally catches up with her. He raises his sword to his lips and then to her in a flourish of congratulation. 'I salute you, Zena – you fly like Artemis!'

My attention is caught by a movement on the clifftop above us. The leader looks up. 'My men have returned.'

I can't help remarking, 'The execution must have been a long one. Or did they torture the helots first?'

Buckling on his breastplate, he replies, 'You are behind the times, Wolf Eyes. We are recruiting, not executing now. That's why you're coming with us.'

Instinctively I draw close to Zena. 'No!'

But she pushes me towards the leader. 'Yes, Lycon!'

'I'm not leaving you—'

'I'll find my way!'

From above, one of the men chucks a flask of water down to the leader. He passes it to me, saying, 'She will find her way. Sparta is not Athens, Wolf Eyes!'

Zena hands him his sword belt. 'Before I go, you owe me your real name, Swordsman – I'm faster than you, remember?'

He buckles on his sword and she passes him the fierce helmet with its cockade of black horsehair. Tucking the helmet beneath his arm with a slight smile and a small bow, he replies, 'Zena, daughter of Zeus and envy of Artemis, my name is Leon.'

A couple of years later, when I had completed a crash course in reading, writing, philosophy and mathematics, I remembered Leon's flowery words. He'd have been ruthlessly mocked by his fellow students, as being the opposite of laconic. You see, this land where we live is called Laconia (Sparta is the city state). And we Laconians are known for not using twelve words when two will do. But I think Leon was already in love with Zena after only two nights' acquaintance. And love gives you either verbal constipation or incontinence; I had always suffered from the former and it was the latter with the head of Sparta's secret service.

*

There's a temple to Hephaestos on the Acropolis in Athens. There aren't any in Sparta and it must have suited Leon well that the god of fire has a low profile here. Because the role he was forging for me in the Krypteia was not that of any ordinary blacksmith. There were plenty of fireworkers around who could knock up your ploughs and other farming tools. But far fewer who understood the art of creating armour and weapons so strong they could practically make you immortal.

Problem was, Pyro was getting on and needed an apprentice who could do more than pump bellows like his life depended on it (Pyro wasn't his real name – when you're in the Krypteia there's a code word for nearly everything). Leon must have seen something about me that wasn't my shrivelled leg; and it wasn't just the strength in my back and arms. From the moment Pyro grasped my hand with a grip that could shatter rock, I was on fire.

By the end of the first week I had hammered out a muscle breastplate that Pyro growled was 'passing good'; next came a helmet, which I burnished until it shone like the sun in the firelight of the forge. A shield was my next baptism of fire. Pyro says a Spartan could lose his helmet or breastplate with impunity but would be disgraced if he lost his shield: because it doesn't just protect him, it protects the entire line.

Then Pyro showed me the short, stabbing sword. It reminded me of Leon's. And Pyro told me how Spartans' knowledge of human anatomy taught them not to waste energy by slashing wildly, but to thrust beneath the armour, aiming for the internal organs of the abdomen, the femoral arteries of the inner thighs, the groin or the throat, to make short work of dispatching the enemy.

And all this time I was also learning about the special mix of metals that make Spartan armour and weaponry so terrifying. I learned why their manufacture is exclusively the preserve of the Krypteia. The metal is all imported, with ships coming in at dead of night and being met by a Krypteian patrol. Some precious metals are involved, such as gold and silver, but they're reserved for jewellery and thrones. Tin is almost as priceless because it's just as scarce – but essential for armoury and weaponry. I have no idea where all this stuff is mined, or even where they unload the ships. Pyro says gruffly, 'What you don't know won't hurt you, Wolf Cub.'

Leon would not have agreed with that. Part of his plan for my new career was that I got at least as well educated as his comrades. So when I wasn't hammering out breastplates I was sitting with a tutor – sometimes two, to really bang it into my head – learning to read and write. This didn't take long as I needed those skills for my work with Pyro. The mathematics came in very handy too, in getting expensive metal plate accurately measured. Then came the philosophy. Or rather, then came Xenophon.

*

During my two-year crash course I would catch up on a lot of work at night, once the day's studies were done. The forge was not so volcanically hot as it was in the daytime and I could work with the doors open, safe in the knowledge that the Krypteia's curfew would protect my valuable metals from thieving hands.

In the early hours of the morning, I'm bashing furiously at a breastplate, sweat pouring off me, when in between the hammer blows I hear the sound of horses' hooves. From the shadows, Leon appears minus his armour, riding a fine Thessalian stallion and leading another one. You don't see many horses in Sparta as it's an expensive business to run a warhorse. Thessalians are a splendid breed, well-muscled in the shoulders and with strong, curving necks and slender legs; they also have a kindly eye. Leon's animals baulk at the heat and smell of the fire. Talking to them in his quiet voice, he jumps down and leads them to a water trough a little distance away. I put the breastplate to one side and join him. Stroking the smooth chestnut flanks of his mount, he hands me the reins of the smoky grey he's leading. 'Have you been on horseback?'

I shake my head. Still gently stroking his horse, he says, 'Then meet Balios and Xanthos.'

'The immortal horses of Achilles…'

'As your lessons will have taught you. Sparta's cavalry is sorely in need of improvement – including their armour. I want you to help me. And we will take as our teacher the man who was the mightiest warrior the world has ever known. He was also a fine historian. And the ultimate master of the art of horsemanship.'

'I thought Xenophon was a philosopher…'

'A follower of Socrates, yes. But so much more besides. The man is practically a god.'

'Is… you mean, he's still alive?'

'We will come to that!'

And so in the early hours of that morning, my military

education began. Starting with the horse side of things. These animals are way bigger than sheep, so you can't wrestle them to get them to obey you. They're also at least as timid as sheep, so you have to speak softly to them and never get angry. All this takes time. Dawn was breaking over Mount Taygetos before Balios would allow me to swing onto his back without taking a giant leap sideways like a wolf had his throat. And it was three weeks before he and I knew each other well enough to ride out onto the mountain with Leon and Xanthos. But it was then that I began to understand the precious bond that a rider can build with a horse.

The test comes when Balios and I are following Leon along a narrow mountain pathway and he suddenly motions us to stop. I can see Xanthos trembling, tossing his head, eyes rolling. And I can feel Balios sweating and tense beneath me. Then I see the snake. Maybe four feet long with orange-red markings and a V mark on its head. I know it's a harmless leopard snake. But the horses don't know that: their deepest instincts are urging them to flee, which could send us all straight into the thousand-foot chasm below. I can hear Leon soothing Xanthos, so I just murmur to Balios, 'Easy, easy, Beautiful. It won't hurt us.' And I run a steady hand down his sweaty neck. Terrified though he is, he doesn't move.

With tears in my eyes, I realise the courage of these noble animals, that will take them calmly past snakes and headlong into the hell of battle for the sake of the rider they trust. As we descend into the valley and work off the tension with a gallop, I call to Balios, 'I'm going to make you the finest armour in the world!'

Through the flying mane of Xanthos, Leon calls back, 'Only the best, for the horses of Achilles!'

*

Once I could read proficiently, my tutors brought me all the works of Xenophon that had so far been written. They told me that the great man was indeed still alive and continuing to write in his retirement on an estate bestowed on him by grateful Spartan kings. This estate, given in recognition of his leadership of so many successful Spartan campaigns, is in a place called Scillus near Olympia (sadly nowhere near Mount Olympus, which would have been fitting for a man with such godlike talents and mental powers). I wondered if I would ever meet him, especially once I started making the armour for the cavalry horses. In the meantime, I read Xenophon until far into the early hours, along with, of course, Homer.

I also made myself useful in other ways than metalwork. There was a queue of customers for armour, and some were more loose-tongued than any true Laconian should have been. As though this armourer measuring their chest was deaf/mute as well as lame. Most of the time the chit-chat was about luxury goods that were being smuggled in, against Sparta's strict laws. Some of the wealthier landowners couldn't stomach the austere, military lifestyle that was the ethos of the Spartan state. So I'd hear about how so-and-so's humble-looking house was now graced by a life-sized bust of Athena. Or how what's-his-name's wife was now sporting a gold necklace. I would slip this news to

Leon during our early morning rides. And I soon realised from his unsurprised expression that part of my new role had always been as a well-planted spy for the Krypteia.

One morning I have more serious news. I wait until we're well out into the mountains before nudging Balios alongside Xanthos. I'm not very good at getting my thoughts in order about possibly having overheard treachery against a king. So I chew my lip and stare ahead at nothing in particular. Used to reading silence better than words, Leon says, 'Out with it, Wolf Eyes.'

'Do you know a cavalryman called Hipparchos?'

'Has served Sparta well in the past.'

'It's probably nothing then…'

Leon stops Xanthos and looks at me. 'Good servants can always turn. Especially if they feel that they have not been adequately rewarded. What is he planning?'

'It looks like regicide…'

'Are you sure?'

'No. And it's what he did rather than what he said.' I draw my index finger across my throat. 'He didn't say which king either.'

'In which case, both are under suspicion. I'll need to check our infiltration of their bodyguards.' He pushes Xanthos onwards and into a trot.

Stunned at his matter-of-factness, I ask, 'Does this sort of thing crop up all the time, then?'

'There are upsides and downsides to a diarchy, just like there are with a monarchy. Fine if the two kings work together like blood brothers. Good too when we go to war – one leads the campaign; the other stays behind to rule.'

'Is war on the cards, then?'

Leon laughs. 'War is always on the cards in Sparta. It's what we live for and what we die for. Spartans are the only men in the world where the one break in training for war is war itself – far less hard work!'

I mumble, 'So is the king who's keenest to risk his own life for the state the innocent one?'

Leon doesn't answer. He turns us back towards the town. 'We'll do some horseback javelin-throwing tomorrow. I have a feeling you'll be extremely good at it.'

I heard no more about the conspiracy until a long time after. Except that Hipparchos never came back to collect his breastplate. So I modified it to fit the next customer; he didn't ask any questions.

*

I don't know how Leon worked out that I'd be good at horseback javelin-throwing, but I did quite well with the straw dummies he lined up for me: galloping towards them, chucking the javelin at full speed and galloping on.

Next, he presents me with a moving target, by towing a sack of straw on a long rope behind Xanthos. This is far harder, especially because the sack is not travelling in a straight line – as Leon points out, 'What foe is going to oblige you by doing that?' So it's a complex business of adjusting my horse's speed to the speed of the target, then trying to double-guess which way he's going to swerve. And all the time I'm petrified that I'll completely misthrow and kill Xanthos, Leon or both of them.

He gives me a breather and pronounces himself satisfied with my progress. 'You're developing your ability to get inside your enemy's head. Something you've always had.'

'Have I?'

'Our close encounter on Mount Taygetos? You knew that mentally you would throw me by telling me that Zena wasn't your sister. Then you physically threw me by turning the rules of wrestling on their head.'

I laugh. 'I had no choice! My leg was about to pack up.'

'We need fighters who are prepared to flout the conventions of warfare.'

'Like Xenophon and his art of deceit.'

'We can do no better than to emulate him. Now, a final lesson before we finish today. There comes a time in every battle when you've thrown your javelin and all you have left for a fight on horseback is your sword.'

Leon's words that day, and the final lesson of the day, are still carved into my memory and always will be.

*

One early morning, Leon turns up in full armour, horsehair helmet included, and on Balios' back is a set for me. 'Hand-to-hand combat is what Sparta is about. This is going to be the hardest part of your training, Wolf Eyes.' We ride out to a valley beneath Mount Taygetos and leave the horses to forage. It feels strange, putting on a cuirass that I could have made better to fit me; a helmet that someone else has worn; and finally, taking up a shield that obviously has seen plenty of action, it's so battered. Then, Leon hands me a stabbing sword and a dagger.

Facing me, fully armoured, standing on legs far stronger than mine, with his helmet's fierce horsehair plume, he might as well be Achilles. I say through my helmet, 'Let's admit it, I have absolutely no chance.'

He shakes his head. 'You found a way to defeat me that night on Mount Taygetos. Do it again, Wolf Eyes!'

He feints as though to go for my throat. I raise my shield and quick as a flash his iron blade is on my inner thigh. If this was real, I would now be drawing my last breath as my femoral artery gushes bright blood.

The next time Leon's sword comes my way, I manage to send it flying out of his hand. But I'm too slow; his dagger is at my neck, his arm wrenching my head back to expose my throat for the death blow.

The third time we launch into battle, I scoop up some dirt and throw it at Leon's eyes. Enough gets past the helmet to temporarily blind him, long enough for me to floor him with a kick in the chest and stand with my sword at his throat. 'I'm sorry, Leon – I hated doing that.'

He gets up, dusting himself off and removing his helmet to wipe the dirt from his eyes. 'Don't be sorry for using your brains to win a fight, Wolf Eyes! We'll continue tomorrow. And you can start making yourself a decent set of armour.'

*

It was a full two years by the time I completed my apprenticeship to Pyro. My reputation was growing with the soldiers who came to me to protect them in battle. And along with protecting limbs, I learned something that was more valuable than being the finest armourer in the world. It started when I was taking a delivery of copper. One of the men could only use one hand to carry the load; the other hand was holding his crutch. This man, Meteos, had lost the lower part of his leg in a riding accident. He wasn't old, around forty, and you're expected to work until you're sixty in the Spartan army. Pyro dug out an old wooden leg from the back of the forge and showed me how to adapt it. It was made from a wooden core – ash for hardness, like spears – and leather for the outer skin and fitting straps. It worked so well that Meteos was able to return to his career as a cavalryman.

Turned out that Pyro had knowledge I had never dreamed of. And yet I ought to have known. After all, the fire god Hephaestos was not only an armourer, making Achilles' armour and arms at the request of his goddess mother Thetis; he was also lame, and made himself all kinds of mobility aids, from winged sandals to flying chariots. Pyro, if anything, had even more godlike skills to teach me. He began with my joker leg: making a brace from wood and leather that ran from just below my knee to a wooden sole. And suddenly I was barely limping at all; my leg felt far stronger. He watched my walk closely and made some adjustments. Then he told me to let him know if it rubbed anywhere. It didn't; I still wear it today.

But Pyro's magic didn't stop there. It was early in the morning and I was stoking the forge fire, when two soldiers arrived carrying an injured comrade on his shield. Instantly, Pyro tells me to clean my hands and pick some yarrow. He grows this little plant next to the water trough outside the forge; once, when I had cut myself badly, he used it to slow the bleeding. And he said it had antiseptic properties which can help prevent the wound getting infected. It's also called the Achilles herb; you'll find it in the *Iliad* at the end of Book Eleven.

When I return with the plant, Pyro is examining the man's mangled lower leg. The soldier must be in great pain, but he's never going to show it. Pyro asks the man's comrades when the injury happened; they say, two days ago – it's taken them all that time to get him back here from training in the mountains. Pyro mutters, 'The leg must go below the knee – there's gangrene setting in. If I don't take it off now, he'll lose the whole leg.' The injured man moves his head slightly in agreement, sweat glistening on his forehead. We're all aware of the sickly smell of decay.

I fetch the wounded soldier and his friends some water, and as the temperature in the forge rises ever higher with the morning sun and the roaring fire, Pyro gets to work. First he fits a tourniquet tightly around his patient's thigh. Then he ties off the blood vessels to staunch the bleeding, so that he can do the amputation slowly and carefully. I apply the delicate little yarrow leaves to the wound to keep it free of infection and help slow the bleeding. Pyro explains that all this will also allow him to create a stump that will take a wooden leg more easily. He gives his patient a javelin shaft to grip and a strip of leather to bite on, to help him bear the pain. Then Pyro picks up his saw. What follows are not death blows but life blows: removing the deadly decay.

I think that if my lower leg was being sawn off I would simply pass out; but through all his pain, the soldier watches

Pyro at work, his comrades at his side. On his face is a look of relief and gratitude. He knows that what Pyro is doing is saving his life and very possibly his livelihood. He won't ever again be an infantryman; but, like Meteos with his wooden leg and me with my braced leg, he'll be able to ride a horse.

This wasn't the only amputation that I watched Pyro do. Then came the time when it was my turn to safely tie the blood vessels and wield that weapon of mercy, the saw. And one day those skills would enable me to save the life of someone I loved.

*

One morning, Leon comes round on foot, wearing his crimson Spartan army tunic and cloak. He's brought a set for me. 'We're going to the chariot racing. You can't show up looking like a tradesman.'

The closest I'd ever been to a chariot was when one nearly ran me down in the street; the two horses were foaming and driverless. Now, here we are, sat in tiered seats, watching an entry procession of ten chariots, each one drawn by four prancing horses, with the herald announcing the names of the drivers and owners. The track is a narrow oval, with sharp turns around the posts at either end. Twelve laps. With ten drivers barely in charge of forty manic horses, it looks lethal.

I glance at Leon. He's gazing intently at the chariots as they parade past. We can't hear any of the names; the crowd is way too noisy. Behind Leon, a stunningly beautiful woman has just quietly sat down and is completely focused on the same direction as him. I try not to stare but it's difficult. She looks wealthy, not because of any finery, but because of her calm confidence. Normally, married women in Sparta have short-cropped hair, but her copper-coloured hair is long, worn in a graceful braid on her neck. So maybe she's a widow. Then the woman tenses and at the same moment Leon says, 'There she is, Wolf Eyes!'

For the last two years there had not been a day when after a few hours' exhausted sleep I did not wake up thinking of Zena. When I dreamed, she was always there. In my waking thoughts, I would catch her face in the flames of the forge fire. If I was eating bread I would hope she was getting enough. When Leon and I were riding on the mountain, every swooping swallow made me think of Zena's long legs making light of the miles.

But now that Zena is only fifty feet away, driving that four-horse chariot, I stare like a dying man confronted with a vision of Hades. The shock must have drained all the blood from my face because Leon turns, expecting me to look delighted, and exclaims, 'Lycon, are you ill?'

'She could be killed!'

Leon laughs. 'Zena's not doing this to be killed – she's doing it to *win*! Watch her!'

'I'm not sure I can.'

There's a light touch on my shoulder. I turn, and it's the beautiful woman sat behind us. Leon and I both promptly stand and bow deeply. She smiles and it's like a burst of dazzling sunshine. 'Are you going to introduce us, Leon?'

With another deep bow, he says, 'My lady, it is my great pleasure to present Lycon, my friend and comrade-in-arms. Lycon, this is the Lady Danae – she is Zena's mentor who has taken on Zena's education and her training as a charioteer.'

Hoping I'm doing the right thing, I bow very deeply indeed; perhaps I should kneel. But she smiles again. 'And Zena is showing great promise, I can assure you, Lycon. I would never allow her to compete if I thought otherwise. Now do be seated, both of you – they're under starter's orders!'

Zena has a middle place in the starting line-up. She'll be aiming for a lightning take-off, so she can get ahead and steer into the inside track. This is the fastest lane but also the most dangerous because if a wheel catches the spina – the narrow island in the middle of the oval – or the posts at either end, then may the gods help you. And all the way, the drivers she's ahead of will be after her like ravening wolves, aiming to sabotage her wheels and her horses. If she can just get that all-important start… then I remember Zena beating Leon on the mountain with such effortless ease. She has the added advantage of being the only girl; my maths tells me that she'll have a superior power-to-weight ratio, provided that her chariot is as light as it can be while still being strong. And that gets the armourer in me thinking…

When the start gates open, Zena's horses seem to take flight. She must have been practising hundreds of standing starts to get off the line like that. Within seconds, she's grabbed the inside lane and she's calling to her horses to slow them for the turn. The nimble animals dance round the pole and put on incredible acceleration again for the straight. Already she has a two-length lead over the nearest competitor – and with every lap she's still gaining. Leon laughs again as he sees me sitting there open-mouthed.

Zena's rampage continues until she's storming down the final straight, when, without warning, the axle breaks, throwing her into the air. Only sheer bloody-minded determination must have kept her hanging on. For a few seconds, the wheels are still attached but horribly tilted inward. Without changing pace, the horses thunder across the finish line and the chariot splinters. As it disintegrates, Zena leaps from the wreckage, holding the reins, and sprints through the dust behind the gradually slowing horses. They halt. She hugs them one by one and waves to the spectators. The entire arena erupts as the crowds stand, roar, throw flowers and embrace total strangers.

*

Lady Danae invites Leon and me to eat at her house that evening. Leon and I ride out to her estate, admiring the manege where Zena practises those explosive standing starts. Xanthos and Balios whinny at the stallions in the fields. Leon comments, 'Lady Danae breeds racing horses; they're in hot demand from the equestrian classes but she keeps the fastest ones for Zena.'

'She needs the best chariots as well as the fastest horses. Far stronger, to withstand the speed she goes at.'

'And the fire of your forge will build those chariots, Wolf Eyes.'

TWO

THE SHIELD
OF ACHILLES

I can't remember what we ate at that meal. Through the soft candlelight, all I could do was gaze at Zena. I was so insanely happy to see her again, I nearly forgot to eat. And anytime she wasn't eating, she would be smiling a small, secretive smile at me, which completely demolished any remaining appetite I might have had. She looked radiant, her skin glowing with the health of wealthy people, her hair coiled on her neck in a style similar to Danae's. But best of all, she was smiling at me – something which she rarely did when we were living with Milos and Myra. I guess it was because Zena gave the orders at that time and I just did what I was told. Now, she seems to be looking at my crimson army cloak and tunic with something close to approval.

Once, I see the Lady Danae looking at Leon with something like approval too; or is it more than that? She

27

seems very at ease with him, as though they've known each other for a while. How long, I wonder? Then I'm carried back to that night on the mountain two years ago and Leon's quiet voice: 'She will find her way. Sparta is not Athens, Wolf Eyes!' That's when I realise: Leon has arranged all this. He brought Zena to Danae like he recruited me into the Krypteia. And I have a feeling that Danae has told Zena all about Leon's plans for me as well. She certainly didn't look surprised when she saw me standing with Danae and Leon among the hysterical crowds. In fact, this feels like being invited to someone's birthday party and turning up to find out that it's your own they're celebrating.

Over supper, Leon tells Danae about my plans for Zena's chariot. I go hot with embarrassment as I get the full sun of this beautiful woman's gaze. 'Excellent news, Lycon. Zena cannot continue racing with these flimsy vehicles.'

'No, Lady Danae – she's safer running behind like she ended up doing today.'

'Just as well that you can run so fast, Zena.'

She flashes Leon a grin at his reference to her outrunning him that night. And I'll bet he's told Danae about that as well, selflessly blowing the trumpet for her protégé.

Danae's dazzling eyes are still fixed on me. 'There is someone I know who can be an invaluable advisor to you, Lycon. He has been helping me train Zena to win races; and he has already commented that she needs a far stronger chariot.'

My heart somersaults. 'Do you mean Xenophon?'

'The Master himself.'

*

Soon after that, Leon excuses us. Danae smiles. 'Of course. I know that the night is a long way from over for you both, Leon.'

This is news to me; I'd been planning to put in a few more hours' reading of you-know-who when I got back to the forge. As we trot through the estate past the quiet paddocks, Leon says, 'If you're going to meet Xenophon, you need to see what he's been doing for the cavalry.'

Half an hour later, we're in foothills of Mount Taygetos where I've not been for two years; and this is not the scenery that I remember. From what I can make out in Selene's cloud-flitting light, it's a cavalry assault course, with ditches dug and stone walls erected on the precarious lower slopes of the mountain. Trees have been felled to create barriers as wide as they are high. The ruins of an old shepherd's hut have created a chicane that could be disastrous taken too fast. Even a sheep pen has been used, in a right angle that you have to jump into, turn sharply and then get up enough speed to jump out of. Leon urges Xanthos up the slope to the side of the course. 'We've just time before they arrive.'

Balios and I have jumped ditches and fallen trees before, but not at night, at full gallop on a downhill slope. Then I think, he trusted me with that snake – it's my turn now.

At the top of the course I'm expecting that we'll follow Leon and Xanthos down. But Balios has other ideas. He turns into Pegasus, swooping past Xanthos and heading for the first ditch with his hooves barely touching the ground. It's then that I realise – he's enjoying himself and knows exactly what he's doing; so I give him his head and twine my fingers in his flying mane. In some ways it's a good thing to have a rubbish leg, because I've had to learn to ride almost solely through balance rather than clinging on.

Balios pirouettes through the ruined hut and skims the felled tree in a wonderful stretched leap. He flies a stone wall without missing a pace and takes an exuberant bound into the sheep pen; coming out of the L-shaped turn, his acceleration almost shunts me off, but I manage to get my weight forward in time for the jump out. Now he's galloping almost flat out, merely lengthening his stride to take in an eight-foot-wide ditch that I didn't see until we were over it.

As we reach flatter ground he doesn't slacken the pace but heads straight for a water trough, stops dead and buries his nose in it. I slide gently headfirst down his neck and into the water – on purpose, of course. Leon canters up on Xanthos. 'You'd better get back on board before the master shows up – he'll send you down again!' No sooner have I re-mounted than we turn to watch an armoured rider taking the downhill slope at a breathtaking speed, one hand holding the reins, the other a javelin. Selene's light glows on the pale flanks of a magnificent white charger. Balios and Xanthos look on, ears pricked, like they too know they are watching the master. Leon says, 'Golden Rule Number One for the cavalry commander: never ask your men to do something you cannot do extremely well yourself. Now, we had better move out of the way.' I can hear the light hooves approaching, the horse snorting quietly with each stride. The rider's arm is back, aiming the javelin. It's then that I notice the single scarecrow stuffed with straw just beyond the trough.

Before I can look back, there's a whistling, a thud and the javelin is deeply embedded in the dummy. At the same time, at the top of the course, a trumpet blasts a command and Xenophon's cavalry hurl themselves at the slope. Leon jumps down, runs behind the water trough and drags out five more dummies, lining them up six feet apart. The master lets his horse briefly drink from the trough then moves to watch with us, eyes hooded beneath the helmet.

Seconds later, a javelin whistles through the dark and hits a target. The armoured rider doesn't stop but gallops on to start forming a line at the end of the course. Thick and fast they come now, until all thirty riders have stormed the course, hit their targets and lined up to stand motionless at attention. At some unnoticeable command, Xenophon's white charger does a beautifully collected walk towards the line and stops, neck arched and perfectly still, without even a tail swish. We watch, spellbound, as the horsehair crest on the master's helmet moves ever so slightly. The voice is strong and melodic. 'Men of the Fourth, there was some hesitation through the ruin. You may retrieve your weapons. Be sure to care for your horses well on your return.'

Leon has picked up Xenophon's javelin and hands it to him before remounting Xanthos. The master's helmet turns briefly in our direction to acknowledge. Then he nudges his white horse from a standstill straight into a canter and disappears into the now-moonless night.

*

As I slide off Balios outside the forge and hand the reins to Leon, he says, 'You could be receiving a visitor soon.'

'I'll start tonight.'

I do make a start that night, but as I'm too tired to do anything but sleep, it's in my dreams. I'm watching a mighty Greek warrior using his shield to fend off the slashing blows of his opponent. In the dream I can hear the clashing of iron on bronze. And I have a feeling that this is the legendary Achilles, the finest warrior in the army besieging Troy. Achilles, whose armour was forged by Hephaestos the fire god and given to him by Thetis, his goddess mother.

I wake in the early light of dawn and roll off my bench to pick up the shield I've been working on for the past three days. The thick concave wood base is overlaid on the outside with a layer of bronze and on the inside with leather; suddenly I'm looking at Zena's chariot. If I can put the shield of Achilles in front of her, with strong side panels of the same design, all joined securely together, and if I can then use this tough shell to brace the axle against the shocks of high-speed galloping…

There are so many other improvements I can make to the fragile chariots she's been racing with. Bigger wheels, with six spokes instead of four, positioned at the rear of the chariot instead of the centre, to shift the driver's weight away from the axle and onto the pole and yokes. And I can make these larger wooden wheels strong, with iron tyres.

But what is all this going to do to the weight? Then I think, perhaps I'm fussing too much about weight. Zena is probably two thirds the weight of her male competitors, and she has the most powerful horses. All the same, a heavier chariot will be slower on tight turns than a lighter one: or will it? Could it be more stable? Especially if I position the wheels wider apart? Then I start thinking about the harness. I noticed Zena's horses throwing their heads around at times. Is there a bridle and bit that will keep their heads down and their weight on their back legs? So many questions! The only answer is to get a prototype built and test it to destruction.

Through the fevered days and nights that follow, I barely eat or sleep. At first, there's just one setback after another. Then Pyro hears me cursing and comes up with solutions that I could never have thought of. But his best idea comes when we're surveying the almost-complete chariot, with its bronze panels. 'You'll want to decorate these?'

'Well, yes, but…'

'What with?'

'I wondered about a winged horse on each of the side panels and Artemis on the front? But…' Before I can protest my total lack of experience in something of this scale, Pyro has swept me up in the most challenging metal-working project I've ever attempted.

Ten nerve-wracked days later, I'm putting a final burnish to the panels in the early hours of the morning, when I hear a horse's hooves. Leon swings off Xanthos and takes him to the water trough. Then he pulls two sets of chariot harness from the horse's back and brings them into the forge. 'A present from the master.'

I look closely at the bits and nosebands. 'What did he tell you about them?'

'He said you would know as soon as you saw them.'

'This will keep the horses' heads down, won't it?'

'And their weight on the hind legs, where the traction comes from.'

'We'll need all the traction we can get. This bit of kit is quite a lot heavier.'

Leon walks slowly round the chariot, taking in the figure work on the panels. 'The master's put the horses on a special diet to build their strength. They're eating better than Zena.'

'With these harnesses, we'll be ready to test a two-horse team by tomorrow.'

'That's just the news he wants.' Leon turns to go, then, with a slight smile, 'Your Artemis, Wolf Eyes…'

'Yeah, I know – room for improvement?'

'By Zeus, don't change anything! It would spoil the likeness to Zena.'

*

On the way out to Danae's estate, Leon drives while I ride Balios beside him and watch the horses closely. I decided to use extra padding to get the yokes to fit comfortably behind their withers. This, combined with the attachments to the oval breast bands, should spread the load evenly over their shoulders and prevent the yokes from slipping backwards. The two stallions are trotting happily enough. If the harness was uncomfortable they'd have kicked the chariot to pieces by now.

As we clear the town and reach open country, Leon gently pushes the horses into a canter. Their heads go down and they're using their hind quarters well; hopefully the new bridles will be as effective at a gallop. We've enough room to try a circuit to get an idea of just how good or how bad the turning circle is; Zena won't thank me for slowing her down around the spina. Progressively, Leon tightens the circle and keeps a steady pace. The chariot's big wheels take the uneven ground well and the iron tyres are gripping like I hoped they would. But let's not get too hopeful too soon. Sweating as the sun clears the horizon, I know that this little exercise is nothing compared with the high-speed manoeuvres to come.

We arrive to find an archery contest in progress. In Zena's large practice manege, ten targets have been arranged in a circle facing outwards onto the racetrack. The distance between targets and track is around a hundred yards. Armoured bowmen are warming up by aiming at a further target right at the top of the field. Watching them, on horseback, are Danae and Zena, and with them is the master, fully armoured as before, on his white charger. I have never felt so nervous, but Leon drives calmly up to them and brings the Achilles chariot to a smooth halt.

Zena jumps off her horse, hands the reins to Danae and walks briskly over to us, her eyes bright. I can see a smile on Danae's face as she takes in the Artemis figure. But beautiful is as beautiful does; the test is yet to come. Zena greets her horses and climbs aboard. Leon hands her the reins and comes to stand next to me and Balios. Weapons lowered, the bowmen are standing to attention, looking at the chariot and its driver.

Zena begins with a gentle trotting circuit, followed by a canter. Seemingly satisfied with the general setup, she comes to a halt and waits until her two stallions are completely still, ears pricked forward, waiting. I'm hardly expecting a start like that race as she has a team half the size. How wrong I am. At a command so soft I can hardly hear it, the two animals go from a standstill into a leaping gallop that reaches full speed in fifty yards. Dust is flying up from the big wheels and the sun flashing on bronze as she completes a first circuit and this time, barely losing any speed, makes a tight turn like she has to do on the racetrack.

The stallions power out of the turn as though the chariot isn't there and thunder on round the circuit. They're going at a speed at least as fast as the race. I had hoped for this: that the momentum of the heavier chariot, and its greater stability, would actually make it easier for those fiery stallions to pull. After three high-speed circuits, Zena slows them gently to a walk, talking quietly to them, and brings them to a halt next to the master's horse. He says nothing, but there's that slight nod of the fierce horsehair crest.

On this command, a bowman joins Zena in the chariot and she sets off again round the circuit at a canter. Now I can see that Xenophon has been training Sparta's archers as thoroughly as her cavalry. As they come within range of each target, the bowman whips an arrow from his quiver and fires: bullseye, again and again until all ten targets have been hit. Now Zena increases the speed, and it's the same relentless accuracy. I must have been staring like an idiot, because Leon looks at me with a smile. 'He can hardly miss with the master looking on, can he?'

Finally, Zena lines up the Achilles chariot opposite the target at the top end of the field. That quiet word, and the horses leap into full gallop straight at it. As soon as the bowman has fired, Zena veers the chariot away in a breathtakingly tight curve and they gallop clear. Leon says approvingly, 'Shock and awe charge. You've built us a fine war machine, Wolf Eyes.'

The rest of the day is taken up with every single bowman doing the same rigorous tests as the first, with regular changes of horses. For each run, Zena is the tireless charioteer. And to my huge relief, the Achilles chariot handles it all. My heart is thumping after the bowmen have all departed, Zena and Danae have gone inside, and Xenophon rides over to me and Leon. He removes his helmet and I see a broad, generous brow and penetrating grey eyes. The voice is as strong and melodic as when I first heard it on the cavalry assault course. 'This is the chariot that Sparta needs, Lycon. You will be given the authority and the means to produce many of them.'

*

Xenophon was as good as his word. Sparta became a city of warfare production with hosts of forges springing up around Pyro's. He and I were kept busy training up armourers and metal workers far into every night. With Xenophon's advice, we developed and tested the horse armour too. From the frontlet over the brow and nose to the breastplate and thigh pieces, it had to be light but strong, and comfortable for our brave stallions to wear. We also increased the size and thickness of the saddle cloth so that the horse's vulnerable belly would be better protected. This in turn would provide better protection for the cavalry and the mounted archers, whose numbers were being steadily increased every day.

Leon brought us a steady supply of new armourer recruits from the helots he and his troops found roaming Mount Taygetos at night. He was also selecting the best potential infantrymen. He told me that the ones who were most fearless about breaking the curfew often made the best soldiers. They just needed to be recompensed with land, instead of executed as traitors.

The military were rewarded in other ways too. On the advice of the master, Sparta's two kings instituted regular competitions, with rich prizes for wrestling, running in full armour over the distance of enemy archer fire, javelin-throwing, hand-to-hand combat, archery and chariot racing across bruising courses. And I found myself working, not at the forge full-time anymore, but more and more often side by side with the head of the secret service who found me and Zena on Mount Taygetos, more than two long years ago.

*

One early morning, Leon and I are riding out on the coastal clifftop, wearing plain tunics rather than crimson. He points downwards, towards a small fleet of triremes beached on the sand. 'This is Xenophon's next project. He has shown us how to improve our cavalry, our archers and our chariots. But he says Sparta's greatest weakness is its navy.'

'What's the problem?'

'Numbers. We've not been replacing the ships we've lost; we need a massive building programme.'

'Is he anticipating an enemy invasion?'

'He says history has a depressing habit of repeating itself. Some kind of invasion in the near to medium-term future is inevitable; the question is, from whom? Which is where you come into it, Wolf Eyes. Can you swim?'

Half an hour later, the horses tethered and grazing above a quiet bay, we find out that I can't swim. I just don't seem to have the co-ordination to keep moving through the water; as soon as I launch myself, I sink like a stone. Leon says, 'You're thinking about it too hard. Imagine that I'm some waster who's insulted the woman you love. He thinks he can escape from you by swimming.' He hurls himself into the Aegean in a powerful front crawl. Choking more on rage than on saltwater, my arms like flails and my legs like hammers, I catch him in twenty yards and drag him beneath the waves until I can't hold my breath any longer. Spitting water as we surface, he says, 'Have you guessed why you need to be able to swim, Wolf Eyes?'

'I'm to be your spy in Athens, aren't I? And that's going to take a shipwreck.'

THREE

WINE-DARK SEA

Three nights later, our horses are picking their way carefully down a cliff path towards the beach. Selene's light flickers on the waves rolling onto the shore. And shines on the prow-mounted ram of a trireme that is beached there. A troop of Krypteians are unloading a cargo of copper for the armourers' forges. On the return trip across the water for more supplies, I'll be the cargo.

Leon explained during the ride, 'You'll be dropped as near to Piraeus port as they can get. Probably be a swim of a mile or so. You could get a good initial look at things on your way through.'

'Signs of naval shipbuilding?'

'That is what we need to know.'

'And when I hit land and get arrested, I was crew on a cargo ship that was sunk by pirates.'

'They can't disprove any story to do with pirates. What cargo will you say?'

'Pottery? Precious metals?'

'That'll do.'

'So I'm a sole survivor…'

'Who will be put on sale as a slave in the Athens agora.'

'Don't expect I'll fetch much.'

'With your brains and education, you'll be one of the pricier ones – potential tutor for the offspring of a wealthy Athenian family.'

'And I thought they'd want me for my pretty face.'

Leon laughs. 'It wasn't your pretty face that attracted me to you, Wolf Eyes!'

We arrive at the beach as the troop completes the unloading of the copper. I swing off Balios and hand the reins to Leon. With a brief greeting to his men, he turns the horses back towards the cliff path and I climb aboard.

The centre of the trireme has been adapted to carry cargo rather than oarsmen, so they number eighty instead of the usual one hundred and eighty. As all are fully armed members of the Krypteia, young men at their peak of strength and skill, this is still a formidably fast and manoeuvrable fighting machine. One hundred and twenty feet long, capable of up to ten knots even without using the sail, and with its bronze-clad ram, it's not a proposition that any sensible pirate ship would take on. If they are stupid enough to do so, the trireme will simply charge them at speed, spit their boat on its ten-foot beak like a stuck pig and then deploy its lethal crew to throw out the grappling irons, board and finish them off in close-quarters combat.

Leon said that they'd be headed for a landing point some way down the coast from Piraeus to collect the next load of copper. The voyage, skirting the coastline, takes three days and nights. On the second day there's a series of squalls which the oarsmen, rhythmically responding to the beat of their leader's drum, pull powerfully through, the ship cleaving the waves with its ram. Then we burst into brilliant sunshine and the sea turns as blue as lapis lazuli. Flying fish leap alongside us as though for the sheer joy of it. And I allow myself to enjoy it too. With very little idea of what I'm getting into, I relish every moment. Life would be very boring if I was still stuck on the sheep farm. And I know that Zena would be pushing me to do this, like she relentlessly pushes herself.

*

On the third day, the hawklike gaze of the lookout is more than usually directed to the coastline. Damon, the Krypteian commander of the trireme, explains: 'There's a series of small coves on this part of the coast that are favourites for the pirates because they're so easy to hide in.'

'Would they really want to take you on?'

He laughs. 'They'd rather go after an unarmed merchant ship. But they could get a good price for the precious metals we carry.'

'Surely they could work out that if you're going in this direction, you haven't yet picked up the precious metals?'

Damon taps his forehead. 'Pirates are essentially opportunists – not the smartest fish in the sea.'

Around an hour later, the lookout spots not one but two vessels heading for us: one making for the waters in front of us, the other in a flanking movement. Damon grins, white teeth flashing in his dark-tanned face. 'Well now, if they aren't making it so easy for us and so hard for themselves.'

He calls a command and instantly the oarsmen redouble their efforts, our ship putting on a spurt of speed and heading directly for the pirate ship in front. I have no idea what these thieves of the sea were expecting, but they brazen it out until we're almost on them. Then they make another mistake and turn to try and run for it, so they're now broadside onto us – an even easier target. Seconds later there's a crash and a horrible splintering sound as our ram ploughs into their hull with such force that it knocks their ship onto its side. Our oarsmen back row to disengage and Damon turns his attention to our second assailant. They've seen enough and are making off with as much speed as they can.

Damon is plainly enjoying himself, as are the men. These pirates are going to be taught a lesson where the price is their ship, if not their lives. Behind us, pirate ship number one is slowly turning upside down, men in the water clinging to the hull. In front, pirate ship number two is about to get its stern stove in. Then a white flag is run up their mast and men are standing on deck with their hands in the air. This causes more hilarity among the Krypteian crew. Putting on still more speed, the oarsmen power our ram into the rear of the pirates' vessel; there's another searing crash and it's all over for them. Leaving them to their fate, sinking stern first, we go on our way.

Damon tells me that pirate attacks happen on an almost daily basis in the Aegean. With all those small islands and tiny coves to hide out in, and so many merchant vessels sailing unprotected, it's nice work if you can get it. He says that successful pirates make so much money they can retire early, buy themselves a farm and some slaves to work it, and live in comfort for the rest of their lives. I guess the unsuccessful pirates are the ones who thought it would be a great idea to attack a Spartan trireme.

Damon also says that there's seldom any need to board the pirate vessels and engage in hand-to-hand combat, because the trireme is such an effective fighting machine. I ask him if it's the same in naval battles. He looks thoughtful. 'It all depends on where you are when you take on the enemy, and what their numbers are. So the Persians have vast fleets which you wouldn't want to challenge in the open sea because their numbers would overwhelm you. But their numbers work against them if you corner them in a narrow channel – especially if you can outflank them.'

I ask Damon if I could take a turn at the oars and he's happy to give one of his men a break. He gives me some tips on effective rowing too, like how not to tire yourself out by trying too hard. All this knowledge, especially about naval strategy against the Persians, is to come in very handy at a later time.

*

It's night slowly giving way to hints of first light; in Selene's waning glow I can just dimly make out the main harbour of Piraeus, when the oarsmen briefly heave to and I slip into the sea. For a moment there's that sinking feeling again. Then I imagine that insult to Zena, see Leon in the water ahead of me and I'm off. There's just a smooth swell, and after sitting on a bench for three days and nights, swimming feels good. As I get closer to the harbour, I change to breaststroke to make less noise. Seeing a couple of fishing boats coming out, I swim underwater to get out of their line of sight. Once inside the harbour, I tread water and look around me.

Around fifty triremes are pulled up on the slipways, and there are doubtless more in the rows of sheds along the dockside. About thirty merchant vessels are waiting for first light to sail. But Damon told me that Athens' main naval harbours are on the other side of the isthmus. It's in these two smaller harbours that any shipbuilding will be going on. Quite how I'm going to pay them a visit is unclear. Especially now that I can see, in the steadily growing dawn light, two guards standing by the gatehouse, sword in hand, looking at my head bobbing up and down in their harbour.

Five minutes later, still dripping, I'm standing in chains being interrogated by the chief of harbour security; I imagine he's the boss because he has two swords. He looks bored when I tell him my pirate story and I wonder how many other castaways have washed up with the same tale. They chuck me into a cell where two other men in chains are sitting on the floor. They barely look up when I arrive. I wonder if they've been beaten. As the sun comes up it starts to get almost as hot as the forge and my throat is dry with thirst. To take my mind off it, I think about Zena tearing around the manege in her new chariot.

Around an hour after sitting in this oven, the door opens and we're on the move under armed escort. Three guards for three prisoners manacled hand and foot seems a bit excessive. Perhaps they're all keen to get a share of the proceeds when we're sold in the agora. Although we must make a sorry sight, dripping with sweat and perishing with thirst; not much of a product for the most sophisticated market in the world.

As we march between the two four-and-a-half-mile-long walls that link Piraeus securely with Athens, I recall what Leon has told me about the Athens agora. It's not just a place where you can buy just about any kind of provisions you want. There are magnificent marble halls housing courts of justice where they try people almost every day for serious crimes; more minor issues are sorted out by a magistrate in a small claims court. In one huge round building, there are government officials on hand twenty-four seven in case of an emergency – they actually eat and sleep there overnight. In the agora, philosophers discuss the meaning of life with their followers; when he lived in Athens before being exiled, Xenophon was a follower of Socrates, listening to him in the agora. And of course, there's the awesome temple to the god of metallurgy; I wonder if I'll ever get a chance to pay my respects at the Hephaestion. Probably not. Slaves don't get many chances.

The sun is blazing when they push us into the slave market. There are some quite young boys and girls there, and an old man who doesn't seem to be taking the heat very well; he's sat on the ground with his head in his hands. I wonder what will become of him. I look at the well-dressed Athenian citizens walking around, chatting with each other. Apart from the slaves there are no Athenian women. Leon has told me about this, too. Women and girl citizens live practically all their lives indoors in their homes. When I think about Danae and Zena, coming and going as they please, pursuing their careers in horse breeding and chariot racing, this seems not just astonishing – it seems cruel.

I'm brought abruptly out of these thoughts when one of the guards gives me a blow to the head and growls, 'Keep your eyes to yourself, scum!' So I stare at the ground until he turns away, then cautiously go back to crowd watching. My attention is caught by a man with a broad forehead and pleasant, open expression; he's with a grey-haired friend, walking slowly down the line of slaves. When he sees the old man sat on the ground, he calls over one of the guards and tells him to bring the man some water; his quiet, well-moderated voice reminds me of Leon. Then he gets to me. Not wanting another thump on the head, I lower my eyes. I hear his friend say, 'He looks lame, Philemon.' I bite my lip to hide my annoyance.

'Let him speak for himself. What is your name, young man?'

'Lycon, sir.'

'And does that leg give you much of a problem?'

'It slows me down a bit, sir. But I can wrestle, swim and ride a horse.'

'Can you, indeed.'

The friend comments, 'He speaks well. It's worth asking, Philemon.'

The quiet voice says, 'You may look me in the face, Lycon – I won't bite. Do you know what I am about to ask you?'

I look up into piercing but kindly grey eyes. 'With respect, sir – do you wish to know if I can read and write?'

*

An hour later, I'm sitting in the kitchen of Philemon's house, with a plate of bread and cheese and a flask of water in front of me. I've had a wash and been given a new tunic. And I've been shown the small room beneath the roof terrace where I'll be sleeping, sharing with the cook, Tiro, who's watching me eat with a pleased expression.

Sniffing my feet with interest, and hoping for some stray crumbs, is the family dog, Xerxes: a huge, black hairy hound, named after the second Persian king to try and fail to conquer Greece. Tiro says, 'Must be some time since you last ate – you're very thin.' I've never thought of myself as thin because in Sparta, everyone is pretty lean. There's never a lot to eat. But I noticed in the agora that some men carried fat stomachs, and Tiro himself is quite well rounded.

I mumble gratefully, 'Never had such good bread, Tiro.'

His cheerful face beams. 'Make it meself, first thing every two days. Eat up now, then off you go to see the master. He'll tell you what you'll be doing.'

'Will that be in his study?'

'First room on the left after the entrance from the courtyard.'

The master's door is ajar but I still knock and wait to be called in. He's sitting at his desk with a book open in front of him. Tingling, I can see that it's Homer. He gestures at the chair next to the desk. 'Sit down, Lycon. This is not a test. I take great pleasure in hearing poetry read aloud; I would like you to try the first few lines of the *Iliad*.'

It feels very strange sitting not standing in front of my master, and my hands are shaking slightly as I take the book. But at the sight of the words that I know and love so well, my face is hot with excitement.

> '*Sing, O goddess, the anger of Achilles son of Peleus, that brought countless ills upon the Achaeans. Many a brave soul did it send hurrying down to Hades, and many a hero did it yield a prey to dogs and vultures, for so were the counsels of Zeus fulfilled from the day on which the son of Atreus, king of men, and great Achilles, first fell out with one another.*'

Nervously, I look up from the book. My master is smiling, his face almost glowing. 'Ah, you have a fine voice, Lycon. You see, I am what you might call one of the elders of this city, and affairs of state often weigh heavily on me. But hearing this… the worries melt away. And you – you seem to enjoy reading aloud?'

'I've never done it before, sir. But I do enjoy it.'

'Splendid. I may also, from time to time, ask you to take notes for me; I find it taxing to think up speeches and write them down at the same time. Especially when a certain amount of rhetoric is required to bring people round to my way of thinking.'

'I will be honoured to help you, Master.'

He smiles, satisfied. 'Now, for the duties that will take up most of your time. I have a daughter, Lydia. She is thirteen years of age and used to be tutored by her older sister, Sophia, who has now been lost to us through her marriage. I wish you to take Sophia's place.'

'I'll do my best, sir.'

'In addition to reading and writing, what subjects have you been studying?'

'Mathematics, history and philosophy, sir.' I keep quiet about Xenophon, exiled from Athens to my home country.

'She is especially in need of mathematics tuition. It will benefit her when she is herself the manager of a household in a year or so.'

The thought of a teenager taking on the burdens of a wife and mother makes me go cold. I struggle for words. 'Does… does she like music, sir? I'm afraid I'm no good at all in that area…'

'She excels at the lyre – she will enjoy playing to you, and you reading to her. In fact, I think it is time you met her. She is sitting with her mother.'

The sun casts dappled beams into the courtyard as I follow my master outside. Sitting peacefully weaving and talking quietly are a young girl with coiled golden hair and a graceful lady of maybe thirty years, her pale blonde hair showing only slight traces of grey. Lying next to the small household well, Xerxes is with them in the shade, his large head on his paws. Philemon calls to them, 'My dears, we have a new member of our household. Come to help you with those troublesome sums, Liddy. And reads poetry like Homer's muse.'

The lady smiles graciously at me, and the girl jumps to her feet, clapping her hands. 'Oh, you must read to me! What's your name?'

I look at my master, but he nods to me to go ahead. Bowing to the golden-haired girl, I say, 'My name is Lycon, Mistress Lydia.'

Her eyes sparkle; they're green eyes, flecked with gold. 'Lycon. That means wolflike, doesn't it, Daddy?'

He smiles. 'You have been attending well to your studies, my dear. And there is a warrior called Lycon in the *Iliad*, is there not?'

'And your eyes are amber, Lycon, just like a wolf.'

Her mother intervenes, 'Lydia, my dear, we must treat our staff gently.'

'It's alright, really, my lady. I had a friend who used to call me Wolf Eyes.'

*

After the family have had their supper, I help Tiro to clear up and sort out various household chores. Then we both head for the little upstairs room, where I'm to sleep in more luxury than ever in my life. After the sheep hut it was the forge, and occasionally roughing it on patrol with Leon and his men. And quite often, in the barracks with the army.

Now, lying on my mattress and staring through the window at Selene in her silver glory, I reflect that I might be in a better position than I thought to fulfil Leon's mission. My master is a statesman, one of the top men in Athens, and he wants me to carry out secretarial duties which sound highly confidential. Perhaps I won't need to check out Athens' shipyards to find out if she's preparing for war with Sparta.

FOUR

'WAR IS MAN'S MATTER'

Hector, The Iliad, Book 6

Philemon is keen for Lydia to start on her mathematics the next morning. As I sit down with her, noticing her slightly crestfallen face, I say, 'If we do mathematics this morning, I'll read to you from the *Iliad* in the afternoon – would you like that, Mistress Lydia?'

She instantly brightens. I continue, 'This morning, I can show you how an armourer uses geometry to shape a shield like Achilles'. And you can draw a design for the shield.'

She claps her hands with delight. 'Oh, I want Xerxes on the shield – like Cerberus!'

'And then you can charm the guardian of Hades like Orpheus did, with your music. I would love to hear you play, Mistress Lydia.'

And so the morning passes pleasantly, while I draw on my experience in the forge with maths and metallurgy. And at lunchtime, my little mistress charms her father with her use of geometry. When we sit down again in Philemon's study, she says, 'You seem to know a lot about armour, Lycon. Will you read to me the bit where Patroclus is putting on Achilles' armour to go out and fight because Achilles is sulking in his tent?'

'He was sulking with good reason, don't you think, Mistress Lydia?'

'Because Agamemnon had demanded his slave girl Briseis, yes. But all those men were being killed and their ships were being threatened by the Trojans, weren't they? I think this was Achilles' chance to show that he was above Agamemnon's egoism!'

I look at my mistress with new eyes. For a thirteen-year-old Athenian girl, sheltered as she is, to make such a penetrating judgement takes me completely by surprise. 'If only he had, the war could have taken a very different turn, Mistress Lydia.'

'Exactly. It was up to the mortals to set an example to the gods who had started the whole thing. The gods were no better than squabbling children who could throw thunderbolts!'

Wondering at such a wise head on such young shoulders, and feeling suitably chastened, I turn to Achilles' loyal and loving friend as he prepares to meet his fate.

'As he spoke, Patroclus put on his armour. First he greaved his legs with greaves of good make and fitted with ancle-clasps of silver; after this he donned the cuirass of

the son of Aeacus, richly inlaid and studded. He hung his silver-studded sword of bronze about his shoulders, and then his mighty shield. On his comely head he set his helmet, well-wrought, with a crest of horsehair that nodded menacingly above it.'

My mistress asks suddenly, 'Did you make armour once, Lycon?'

'Yes, Mistress Lydia.'

'So you were like Hephaestos, the god of fire. Was it hot work, making armour?'

'Very hot!'

'Was bronze the best metal for Patroclus' sword, do you think?'

'That is a very good question, Mistress Lydia. Actually, iron would have made a deadlier weapon, although bronze would have looked better. And it was also silver-studded to shine like the stars.'

She gazes thoughtfully at the drawing of her Cerberus shield, then smiles at me to continue.

'He grasped two redoubtable spears that suited his hands, but he did not take the spear of noble Achilles, so stout and strong, for none other of the Achaeans could wield it, though Achilles could do so easily. This was the ashen spear from Mount Pelion, which Chiron had cut upon a mountain top and had given to Peleus, wherewith to deal out death among heroes.'

'Did you make spears too, Lycon?'

'Yes, Mistress Lydia. They were always ash, like that of Achilles, with iron heads.'

Xerxes pads heavily into the study and flops down next to Lydia's small, sandalled feet, giving one of them a lick; she giggles and leans down to stroke him. 'He's so big I could ride on him. Let's have the next bit about the horses, Lycon. I love that bit!'

I love that bit too, as it takes me back to memories that I will always carry with me.

> *'He bade Automedon yoke his horses with all speed, for he was the man whom he held in honour next after Achilles, and on whose support in battle he could rely most firmly. Automedon therefore yoked the fleet horses Xanthos and Balios, steeds that could fly like the wind.'*

Lydia says dreamily, 'Fly like the wind. That's Pegasus, isn't it, Lycon?' She picks up her lyre and runs her fingers gently over the strings; they ring softly, like an echoing Aeolian harp.

I say very quietly, 'There are some real horses that can make you feel like you're flying, Mistress Lydia.'

She puts down the lyre and looks at me, green eyes aflame. 'I knew it! And you've ridden them, haven't you?'

So I tell her about Balios, one of the horses of Achilles. I draw her a picture of his beautiful curving neck and noble head. And I explain how it took us a while to get to know each other. But how, once we trusted each other, he would take me flying down a mountain with his hooves barely touching the ground, effortlessly leaping everything in his path.

She picks up the lyre again. 'I'm going to make up a song about flying horses. You mustn't listen until it's done!'

'I'll go help Tiro. Is Xerxes allowed to stay?'

'Only if he doesn't keep licking my feet!'

I kneel down next to the hairy monster. 'You hear that, Xerxes?'

A quiet snoring is the only reply. Along with Lydia's, 'So he can stay.'

For the rest of the day, the house echoes to the singing of Lydia's lyre and her crystal voice. When Philemon returns, in time for supper for once, Tiro tells me, Lydia regales her parents with her composition and is asked to play it again and again. It's hauntingly sweet and wistful, with words full of wonder. I can still hear the echoes in my head, many years on. May they never leave me.

*

The next day, I'm waiting at table when Lydia's sister Sophia and her husband come to lunch. Sophia has golden hair like her little sister and looks barely two years older than Lydia. Accustomed to the way we do things in Sparta, where women can marry only when they reach the age of twenty and are trained in a fitness regime similar to that of boys and men, I feel a sense of shock seeing that Lydia's sister is expecting a child. With her slight frame such a contrast to Zena's athletic body, I wonder how Sophia will find the strength to withstand the trauma of childbirth.

Philemon and his son-in-law are served in my master's study, where they are probably discussing politics, while the mother eats with her daughters in the dining room. After their meal the ladies retire to the courtyard to much chatter and laughter. And happy though they obviously are, I can't help thinking of what Zena and Danae would be doing now. Instead of being closeted within the walls of a city dwelling, Zena would be practising standing starts with her new chariot and Danae's Thessalian stallions, and galloping around the manege at unimaginable speeds. Or the two of them would be riding out together, looking for some fun. Leon told me not long before I left for Athens that Danae had asked Xenophon to show them how to tackle the cavalry assault course, which he duly did. I teased Leon that at this rate, it wouldn't be long before girls were recruited into the cavalry. His response was one that I had to agree with: 'It's dangerous enough bearing children without having to fight wars as well!'

*

The following morning, my master gives me instructions which immediately put me on alert. 'I need you to accompany me to the naval shipyard and make notes. I am to prepare a report for the assembly.'

We ride in Philemon's carriage pulled by two mules. Progress is slow, but it allows me to cautiously gather as much advance information as I can. 'Is this a new shipbuilding programme, Master, or is it simply replacing triremes that have been lost or become too old?'

Far from being suspicious of my curiosity about Athens' shipbuilding, my kindly master warms to my interest. 'It is both, Lycon. Athens has always taken pride in her navy and scored many great victories. As a result, many of the triremes are quite battle-scarred and need replacing. Which we are doing with larger vessels that can carry more marines and achieve even faster speeds.'

'And you are increasing the size of the fleet, sir?'

As the naval shipyard looms in sight, and guards come forward to check our credentials, Philemon continues, 'Our fleet has always been critical to Athens' safety. We need to be prepared for enemies who look across land and sea and find in us a rich target for conquest.'

As we're escorted to the quayside by the chief overseer, I turn over Philemon's words in my mind. They're about self-defence, not attacking Athens' neighbours. But intensive shipbuilding is definitely well underway. In the sheltered, northward-looking harbour are hundreds of triremes in various stages of construction. I end up with very precise figures, as this is the purpose of Philemon's visit. He is to report to the assembly on shipbuilding progress: how many new triremes are ready to put to sea, how many are a work-in-progress, the total size of the planned fleet and what it is all going to cost the treasury.

On the way back in the carriage, Philemon seems satisfied with progress. And I am spurred on by curiosity to find out more about Athens' war-making capability. 'Is Athens looking to strengthen her military as well as her navy, Master?'

'A good question, Lycon. One might assume so. But most of our army is part-time – not like Sparta's. The men have their land and their families to look after. When a war is declared, they are generous in giving themselves and their resources, especially if they are cavalry. But it is a very different situation to Sparta, where the army only ceases training to fight a war.'

Leon's words echo in my head:

It's what we live for and what we die for.

*

Several weeks on, Lydia's mathematics skills are beginning to outstrip mine. She starts to read the *Iliad* aloud to me, and she begins to write lyrics for the heroic scenes. They don't have the yearning of the winged horse song, but their technical brilliance is dazzling. I wonder if Lydia's father would allow her to teach the lyre. I'm not sure if that kind of thing is done in Athens, where girls and women are so shut indoors. But she has such gifts that it seems an awful shame that they can't be shared. I think about Danae and Xenophon training Zena to win races in front of thousands, when Lydia's beautiful voice can only be heard by her family; and it makes me very sad.

One night, Lydia and her mother have retired to bed when my master calls me into his study. I stand before him respectfully, but he gestures to me to sit near him. His face is worn with affairs of state; but he is also animated. 'Lydia has told me how much she enjoys reading the *Iliad*, Lycon. Would you read this passage to me? There is much that I would like to dwell on there. And it will help me with my address to the assembly tomorrow.'

I know this passage from Book 6 so well. I used to read it a lot because Zena and I don't know who our fathers and mothers were, and I don't expect we ever will.

I look at the familiar text, with the mighty Hector in his final moments as a tender father:

'He stretched his arms towards his child, but the boy cried and nestled in his nurse's bosom, scared at the sight of his father's armour, and at the horsehair plume that nodded fiercely from his helmet. His father and mother laughed to see him, but Hector took the helmet from his head and laid it all gleaming upon the ground. Then he took his darling child, kissed him, and dandled him in his arms, praying over him the while to Zeus and to all the gods. "Zeus," he cried, "grant that this my child may be even as myself, chief among the Trojans; let him be not less excellent in strength and let him rule Ilius with his might. Then may one say of him as he comes from battle, 'The son is far better than the father.' May he bring back the blood-stained spoils of him whom he has laid low and let his mother's heart be glad.

'With this he laid the child again in the arms of his wife, who took him to her own soft bosom, smiling through her tears. As her husband watched her his heart yearned towards her and he caressed her fondly, saying, "My own wife, do not take these things too bitterly to heart. No one can hurry me down to Hades before my time, but if a man's hour is come, be he brave or be he coward, there is no escape for him when he has once been born. Go, then, within the house, and busy yourself with your daily duties,

*your loom, your distaff, and the ordering of your servants;
for war is man's matter, and mine above all others of them
that have been born in Ilius.'*

Philemon says reflectively, 'War is man's matter, is it, Lycon? Then I wonder about peace. And that brings me to tomorrow's address.' He provides me with writing materials and, occasionally pacing up and down, starts to formulate a speech, pausing between sentences to let me keep up. As I listen and write, I stare at the words in front of me, my thoughts tumbling around in my head like boulders hurtling down a mountain.

'Men of Athens, this is a time when to do nothing is not negotiable. If we do nothing we will bitterly regret it, if, that is, we are left alive to regret anything. We have now had reports from three reliable sources that the King of Persia is planning to invade with an army so vast that its like has never before been seen on this earth. This invasion will not, as in the past, be preceded by a visit from ambassadors giving us the opportunity to choose between making gifts of earth and water instead of suffering outright war. We have forfeited any chance of that by our previous treatment of Persia's envoys. So who now should be sending ambassadors? Athens, be in no doubt of that! There is a chance, albeit a very slim one, that diplomacy may yet mitigate this unprecedented threat to our freedom, our democracy and our very lives. I myself will gladly undertake this mission. As you all know, I greatly desire that Sparta be approached to join with us in this. But I also know that there are those amongst you who can never be prevailed upon to agree. Men of Athens, we must not let it be said that, with these storm clouds gathering, we took no action. While we build up our army and our navy, words of diplomacy can at the very least buy us precious time. How infinitely better is that, than hanging our heads in shame at the thought that we did not try the power of the word but merely waited to be put to the sword!'

After making a few corrections, my master reads out the address and I stand to listen to him. In all my life, I have never heard words used to such effect. In Laconia, as you know, we are sparing with words and rightly so in the business of war. But my master is talking about a last-ditch attempt to avoid war through the power of words. He is a man of peace, a very brave man, who is prepared to ride up to the King of Persia's glittering golden throne and sue for peace in the face of all-out, bloody, massacring war. He has the weight of history behind him, where the Persians suffered two humiliating defeats in two massive invasions, the Greeks winning against all the numerical odds. But that was with Sparta and many others in a grand alliance. Now, Athens is proposing to go it alone. My master looks at me as he concludes his address. 'What did you think of that babble, Lycon?'

'On your words, I would follow you to the ends of the earth, Master.'

'If they vote it through, I'll need you to come with me to Persia.'

*

With Philemon's eloquence and his courageous offer, the assembly unanimously voted through his journey as envoy from Athens to the King of the Persians. They also voted him a substantial supply train and an armed guard; quite apart from the risk of bandits, his long journey would cross countries which were vassals to Persia, so no friends of Athenians.

At home, there were suddenly tensions that turned this previously tranquil household upside down. Philemon's wife was rigid with fear for his safety and full of reproach that he could venture on such a mission. Soon, they were no longer eating in the same room; Philemon ate alone in his study. Lydia was quieter in our lessons and kept looking for Xerxes to hug. Then one day, I'm reading aloud to her Hector's farewell to his wife and child:

> *'...do not take these things too bitterly to heart. No one can hurry me down to Hades before my time, but if a man's hour is come, be he brave or be he coward, there is no escape for him when he has once been born.'*

At these words, my little mistress bursts into tears, sobbing as though her heart will break.

'Mistress Lydia, shall I bring your mother to you?'

In between sobs, she gasps, 'You're going away, aren't you, Lycon?'

Wishing that I could hug my mistress to comfort her, but knowing a slave can never do that, all I can say is, 'Yes, Mistress Lydia, I'm going away to help your father on his mission.' How I wish I could promise her that I'll return.

But even if the Persian King spares our lives, I know that my path will not bring me back to my master's house. At the thought of this desertion, I feel hot with shame.

Lydia throws herself on top of Xerxes as he lies at her feet. Between muffled sobs, arms round his neck, she says, 'I love you, Lycon. Please don't leave me.' Hearing Lydia's distress, her mother hurries in and takes her daughter in her arms.

I stammer, 'I… I'm so sorry, my lady. We were reading Hector's farewell and—'

She hushes her child's crying. 'You mustn't blame yourself, Lycon. Her father has never left us in all her life; this is terribly hard for her.'

I think to myself, and for you too, my lady. But I say nothing, just bow my head. She sends me to help Tiro in the kitchen while she sits with Lydia and tries to comfort her.

After that, my lady looked on her husband with kindlier eyes, and family meals together resumed. And I wished sadly that it was indeed a longing for her father that had caused Lydia's tears, as her mother had supposed. Not an impossible love for a slave.

*

A few days later, Philemon asks me to check the supplies for the baggage train. He gives me a huge list and directs me to the large open-air shed where the carts are being loaded, then he goes on to the assembly. Inside the shed, sack-loads of grain, dried fruit, cheeses and emergency fodder for the mules are being stacked onto the carts, under the supervision of a government official, an Athenian freeman who introduces himself as Cleon. He grins when he sees the list. 'You'll have your work cut out ticking this lot off!'

I can see what he means; all the sacks look the same. 'Here, I'll give you a guided tour.' He produces his own list and walks me round the carts, telling me what's what, while I scan frantically up and down my list. Everything is present and correct. 'That's really good of you, Cleon – I wouldn't have had a chance without you!' Then I turn to look at the black stallion standing in his loose box at the other end of the shed. A horse that I've been gaping at ever since I arrived, he's so heart-stoppingly beautiful.

Cleon sees me looking. 'Ah, yes. Apparently he'll be joining you on your little jaunt. Come and meet Arion.'

'One of the immortal horses of the gods…'

'If you say so. He's certainly supernaturally fast, to all accounts.'

Arion watches us approach, ears pricked. Large flaring nostrils and the deep chest tell of big lungs and a mighty heart. The dark, intelligent eyes are set either side of a broad, dished brow in a fine, tapering head. Gazing into those eyes, I receive a look in return that seems to touch my soul. I whisper, 'I've never seen a horse like this.'

Cleon runs a gentle hand along the gleaming neck. 'There aren't many Arabians this side of Persia. This fellow's worth his weight in gold; he's guarded night and day.'

Arion's steady gaze holds me as I come up to him. He stands without a toss of the head or a tail swish as I stroke, first his back, then his neck. As I extend my open palm, he drops his soft muzzle into it. Running my hand quietly up his broad brow, I know that I'm making friends with a lion heart, a horse that is not afraid of anything, as long as he has a rider he can trust.

*

Later on that day, in Philemon's study, he asks me about the supply train. 'Everything on the list was there, sir.'

With a slight smile, he asks, 'And was there anything there that was not on the list?'

'The most beautiful horse that I have ever seen in my life, Master. Arion the Arabian.'

'Do you know why Arion will be coming with us, Lycon?'

'If there is news that you need to send urgently to Athens, sir?'

'And if there is news that needs to travel urgently to Athens, how do you feel about being Arion's rider, Lycon?'

'I… can't find the words, Master.'

He smiles again. 'I won't ask how you came to be a horse rider, Lycon. We don't enquire about the past lives of the people who serve us so loyally. But I suggest that when you are not tutoring Liddy, you may wish to further your acquaintance with Arion.'

'Thank you, sir. How many days before we leave for Persia?'

'Four more days before all is ready. In the meantime, letters have been sent ahead to prepare the ground with the King of Persia. Or, as he likes to style himself, the King of Kings.'

My little mistress seems happier now that the family is reunited at mealtimes. She shows a renewed interest in mathematics, if only to please her father as much as possible before he goes away. Between lessons, I take my master at his word and go to visit Arion. And I remember the writings of Xenophon on horsemanship, about how important it is to spend time together. So, in those days before we leave for Persia, Arion and I keep each other company.

One day when I enter the shed, he's lying down in the straw. So I sit down with him, and he moves his head into my lap. There is no experience on earth like the world's most beautiful horse lying his head on your legs, in a position of utmost trust. I'm so close to those huge dark eyes; I can hear his every breath and smell its sweetness from the wheat that he's been eating. This amazing head is heavy, mind, so the blood supply to my thighs has been almost cut off when Cleon brings over some more forage and Arion gets up, shakes himself all over and dives his head into the food.

The next day when I turn up after a maths lesson with my mistress, I decide to give Arion some grooming. Cleon looks at his list and locates the brushes. I pick the finer one, as it's simply bits of straw I need to clean from that gleaming coat. With rhythmic strokes, I move the brush gently from withers to rump. Arion half closes his eyes, like he's enjoying the massage. I hum to him Lydia's flying horse song. When I turn, I see Cleon watching us and grinning. 'Reckon you two were made for each other.'

Two days before we leave, Lydia's sister Sophia and her husband come to eat with the family and the atmosphere is warm and happy. They say to Lydia that she must stay with them while her father is away and they will pamper her until she is quite ruined. My mistress's mother makes playful protest and is invited herself to stay with her daughter and son-in-law. Waiting at table, I watch my master's face carefully; the slight smile is there, and I guess that he is behind these offers of hospitality.

Helping Tiro in the kitchen later, I remark on what a very kind man our master is. He holds out his hand three feet above the floor. 'I were that small when I came 'ere. Found on street. Didn't know 'owt. Bin 'ere ever since.'

'Did you learn from the cook who was here at the time?'

'Got plenty of clips be'ind the ear. But if you screw up baking bread that's what you deserve – waste of good food.'

The next day, the day before we leave for Persia, my lady and my little mistress are packing to go and stay with Sophia and her husband at their villa on the coast. Xerxes is making himself useful, unpacking every garment as fast as they try and pack it. Exasperated, my lady eventually says, 'Lycon, please just take him out of the house or we'll all go mad!'

'My master says I may check the supply train, my lady.'

'Perfect. Take a long time over it, please!'

With a rope around Xerxes' neck to curb his enthusiasm, I set off for the open-air shed where the supply train is being assembled. Cleon waves to me. 'Got another list?'

'No – I'm walking the dog and come to see Arion.'

'Glad you did. He's getting a bit restless, tied up here.'

Arion's eyes are on me from the moment I enter the shed. He gives a deep-throated whinny as I approach, and the thick black tail swishes. How is a horse that was born to fly like the wind going to put up with so much inactivity? My lady's words echo in my head, *Take a long time over it, please!*

I say to Cleon, 'Is his bridle here? And a saddle pad?'

He consults the omnipotent list. 'Should be. Give me a moment.' He rummages in one of the carts.

I look into the endless depths of Arion's dark eyes. No words need to be spoken. I never can find words for him. Cleon comes over with a saddle pad. 'There should be a bridle in there somewhere…'

Easing the saddle pad onto the glossy back, I say, 'We may not need it. Do you like dogs, Cleon?'

He takes the lead off me. Xerxes positively fawns on him. 'Nice chap, aren't you?'

Attaching a short rope to Arion's halter before I mount, I whisper to him, 'I'm very clumsy with this weak leg. I hope you'll forgive me.'

Ears flicking back and forth, he never moves as I grasp his mane and throw myself aboard him. And now I have this magnificent neck curving ahead of me, and this fluid movement of powerful legs beneath, as we walk gently out of the shed and into the morning air of Athens. All I have in my hands is the halter rope. But Leon taught me that only rarely do you need to steer a horse with the reins. It's all down to where you put your weight, and how you use your legs and your voice.

I can feel Arion's pleasure at being out in the fresh air and on the move. As we walk on, I talk to him and see his ears paying attention. I tell him about the long journey we'll be making, and how important it is. How we'll be together.

And how, maybe, we'll have to gallop and gallop for days and days to take a vital message. And all the time we walk, I can sense this colossal energy beneath me.

Through the streets of Athens, Arion attracts many admiring glances. He knows he's beautiful. Arching his neck, he dances at the walk. Those long, flexible fetlocks are used to galloping through desert sand, giving the rider a sense of floating, even at walking and trotting paces. As we clear the town and enter open country, mountains looming to our right, Arion's dancing walk never speeds up. But I know that all I have to do is shift my weight forward and we'll fly. Finally, neither of us can resist.

As I make that tiny shift in weight, the power explodes beneath me. I'm on the back of the wind, a streaming black mane in my eyes. Arion becomes his true self. Born to run, those flaring nostrils breathing air into massive lungs that feed the mighty heart. Lionheart.

I can feel his joy and I'm sure he can feel mine. There is nothing on earth that comes close to this union. If there was such a thing as a second life, I would love to live it as an Arabian. Although I can't imagine that this Arabian would ever want to return as anything other than himself.

In the mid-afternoon, with a quiet contentment, we arrive back at a gentle walk at Arion's lodgings in the shed. He takes long, slow gulps of water from his trough and shudders his coat appreciatively as I brush him down. I take the coarser brush and groom his mane and tail until they shine in dark cascades. He turns his head and blows softly into my ear. The Arabian knows we're off tomorrow, on the longest journey of our lives.

Cleon hands over Xerxes. 'He slept a lot.'

'I'm glad he didn't wear you out! My lady was becoming really fed up with him.'

'Ah, well, he did get to be quite a favourite with the guards. They kept bringing him treats. Must have been quite tiring for him.'

'Thanks, Cleon.'

He gives Xerxes a thumping pat. 'So, tomorrow at dawn – the big day, is it?'

'The big day, yeah.'

He gestures towards the guards stationed around the shed. 'These guys will all be coming with you – plus quite a few more. Bit of an expedition, isn't it?'

'I've never done anything like this before, Cleon. No idea what to expect.'

He shrugs. 'I sent the letter bearers on their way a few weeks back. Hopefully their tidings will have reached the King of Kings by now.'

'And hopefully, they'll still be alive?'

'Who's to say? You just do what you're told and what you can.'

I look towards the end of the barn, where Arion is rolling on his straw bed, and I whisper, 'Tell me, Cleon – have you ever seen a horse as amazing as that?'

Cleon bends to tickle Xerxes behind his ears. Xerxes licks his feet. 'The gods broke the mould after they made Arion, Lycon. You're a lucky man.'

There are times when you feel so lucky that you have to give thanks. On the way home with Xerxes, I remember my lady's instructions to take a long time, so we call by the temple of Hephaestos, god of fire, metallurgy and craftsmanship, next to the agora. There are many potters and metal-working shops nearby. I wonder how the chariot production is going back in Sparta. And what Zena is doing…

Restraining my thoughts from wandering further, I admire the statues of Hephaestos and Athena. The crippled god of fire, next to Zeus' most brilliant child; goddess of wisdom, learning and the arts but also a warrior goddess, shown here with a shield and spear. I kneel, whispering my thanks for all the good things that have happened since I washed up in Piraeus. Then I add, 'May you, kind goddess, care for my little mistress Lydia.' I gaze at her calm, inscrutable face for some minutes, before allowing Xerxes to tow me into the small garden outside the temple. Here he ecstatically roots among the shrubs and trees of pomegranate, myrtle and laurel. Watching him, I hear Lydia's winged horse song breaking in on my memory. The liquid notes of her lyre and the pure crystal of her voice echo in my head all the way back to the house.

*

When we get back, Tiro whispers, 'My lady and the little mistress left this afternoon for the coast. Our master feels it's better that way.'

'Much better than them watching us depart, Tiro. So you'll be dog minding?'

He takes Xerxes' lead and undoes the rope. 'He and I get on well – he knows where the food comes from!'

'Has the master retired to bed?'

'Not yet. He wants you to pop into his study before you go upstairs. And there's some bread and cheese for you in the kitchen.'

Thinking that I have never been so well fed in my life, I knock on Philemon's door. He's prepared a letter which he rolls and stamps with his seal. 'Can you take this to a colleague of mine in the assembly, please, Lycon. He is expecting it. His name is Aristides.' He gives me the address and I'm off, shambling along the twilight streets until I find the large villa on the outskirts of town. I'm shown into a hallway where I stand and wait for a few minutes. During that time, a very pretty girl slave offers to take my document to her master. I shake my head. 'I'm sorry, but my master's orders were precise. I have to hand this document to Master Aristides myself.'

From a room off the hallway, a tall grey-haired man appears; I realise that it's the friend Philemon was walking round the slave market with the day he bought me. Dismissing the girl slave, he approaches. 'Now I know that you are who you say you are, Lycon.'

Bowing, I hand him the letter.

'Thank you. Can we offer you some food before you return home?'

'Thank you, sir, but I am well looked after at my master's house.'

'I do not doubt it. Please tell your master that I will be sacrificing to Zeus tomorrow to pray for his safe journey and safe return.'

When I get back to my master's house and give him Aristides' message, he asks me to remain in his study for a few minutes more. He's looking for a book; when he sits down with it at his desk, I'm stunned to see that it's Xenophon's writings. I thought that the master's books would have been banned in Athens after his exile. Philemon bids me sit down in my usual chair next to his desk; nervously, I do so, wondering if I'm going to be unmasked as a spy who has traded ruthlessly on his generosity. He says reflectively, like when he was putting that speech together, 'You know that I wished for Sparta to be involved with this mission, don't you, Lycon?'

'Yes, Master.'

'You also know that I had to acknowledge the implacable opposition of certain members of the assembly to Sparta being involved?'

'Yes, sir.'

His next words are not the words of a master to his slave. 'What would you say to me if I told you that I still wish Sparta to be involved with this mission, Lycon?'

I pause for several seconds that feel like hours. Philemon pushes Xenophon's book towards me, saying gently, 'I urged you to deepen your relationship with Arion because I greatly admire the writings of Xenophon on horsemanship.'

Finally I find my voice. 'So do I, Master.'

'And you are a Spartan, are you not, Lycon?'

'Yes, sir.'

'Then there is no better companion that I could wish for on this mission!'

FIVE

THE GATE OF ISHTAR

I hardly sleep that night, I'm so astounded by the turn events have taken. A few hours later, as rosy dawn starts to tint the horizon, my master and I are outside the big shed, where mules are being harnessed to the baggage train. Cleon leads Arion up to me; the Arabian has been saddled and bridled. 'I thought you'd want to ride him for the first leg – just so he doesn't think he's being left behind!' Arion's eyes are bright with interest as he watches the hustle and bustle. Philemon is talking to the leader of the cavalry. The fully armed riders are checking their horses' armour and their weapons. One of the mules sets up a loud braying and some of the cavalry horses start to whinny back. But Arion doesn't make a sound; he just takes it in like he's seen it all before. Perhaps he has.

Cleon keeps looking anxiously down the agora, like he's waiting for someone or something else to arrive. There's a bit of a stir, as a boy slave carrying a large basket full of pigeons hurries up to him. He stows the basket carefully on one of the carts and finally we're on our way, processing through the streets of Athens. Citizens going to the agora stop talking to each other and stare at the cavalry with their flashing bronze shields and breastplates and fierce horsehair plumes. An Athenian citizen shouts up at me as I ride my Arabian, 'What's this all about, slave?' The man goes quiet as a cavalry officer points his spear at his head.

Clear of Athens, riding out into open country with mountains to either side, our convoy creates a long cloud of dust that trails behind us. We travel throughout the blazing day. Arion seems to enjoy being part of this adventure; his dancing walk carries us endlessly on as we accompany Philemon's carriage, so that I can care for my master should he need anything. Some of the time, I see Philemon sleeping, and wonder how he can relax with such jolting over the rough surface.

We travel until the sun has sunk down below the horizon, and in the cooling evening the soldiers pitch a camp for the convoy. Their cooks bring Philemon and me some figs, cheese and bread, with watered wine to wash it down. Arion is foraging nearby, and my plan is to sleep with his halter rope tied round my waist.

In the flickering flames of the fire, Philemon's grey eyes look at mine. I take a deep breath. 'May I speak, Master?'

'I am listening, Lycon.'

'You told me last night that you greatly admire Xenophon and you read his books. I… wondered if, once, you knew him? Before he was exiled?'

'Ah, you have a quick mind, Lycon. It is not something that I mention these days for obvious reasons; but before he departed on the expedition of the Ten Thousand, we were firm friends. I would like to think that we still are, many years on from his extraordinary military achievements.'

'Then I can tell you that I have been designing and building a new chariot for Xenophon.'

'So you are an armourer. Liddy said you knew a great deal about armour.'

'Mistress Lydia has a quicker mind than me, sir!'

'But how is it that you can ride so proficiently?'

I tell him about that fateful night when Leon bade me follow him off the mountain and into the Krypteia. How he had me trained as an armourer and educated in reading, writing, mathematics and Homer's and Xenophon's works. How Leon trained me in fighting, horsemanship and cavalry command according to Xenophon's way. And how I began to work with Leon and Xenophon, in their projects for strengthening Sparta's army.

Philemon takes a stick and stirs the fire until the sparks dance. 'So Sparta is arming herself. Does she fear what Athens may be planning to do to her? Is that what Leon sent you to find out?'

I blush crimson with shame and start to stammer.

He shakes his head. 'I would have done exactly the same in his position. And I thank Zeus that Leon did send you to me.'

'So do I, sir.'

'You are now my most valuable ally in this mission, Lycon. If it turns out that the Persian King is indeed planning an invasion, Athens cannot fight it alone. Not even with her former allies. Immediately after you have taken my message to Aristides, you must continue onwards to Sparta – to Leon and Xenophon.'

*

In two weeks of travel we reach the coast, where we must ship our convoy across the water. The Athenian navy has provided three big triremes, modified for the carriages and mules and the cavalry's horses. In addition, four heavily armed triremes are escorting us.

The mules hate going up the gangplanks, which feel hollow and insecure beneath their hooves. They have to be tempted by food and finally smacked on their backsides to get on board.

Philemon looks at me. 'If you and Arion lead the way, you will find that the cavalry horses are minded to follow.' He's right. I don't think that anything can faze my dark charger, as he prances gaily up the boarding plank. The cavalry officers grin as their mounts rush after Arion and bury their muzzles in the fodder awaiting them.

Before Philemon and I board, he asks me to accompany him to the commander of one of the adapted triremes. He introduces us. 'Antilochus, this is Lycon. He was my slave but is now a free man, because he has a vital role to play in the welfare of Greece.'

Stunned at this news, I return the firm grasp of Antilochus as he shakes my hand. He says, 'I was a slave once, Lycon. Welcome, comrade.' He's tall, bearded and dark-haired, and I feel as though I know him.

Philemon continues, 'We are, as you know, Antilochus, on a long journey to sue for peace from the King of Kings. That may not be forthcoming. If it is not, then Lycon here must ride to warn Athens. I need you to be waiting, to take him and his horse back to Greece. The gods being willing, my retinue will follow sometime afterwards.'

Antilochus says steadily, 'We will be there, Master Philemon. We will wait until Hades freezes over.' He grasps my hand again, and I know that I can be sure of this man.

I've heard of many storms that have wracked the sea between Greece and Persia, but Poseidon looked kindly on our ships. The winds were gentle, the waves lightly tipped with curling foam and we had a pleasant voyage. As we disembarked, I shook hands again with Antilochus. He looked at Arion's proud head and shining eyes. 'You have a horse of the gods, my friend. I hope well to see you both again and take you home to Greece!'

*

Climbing back into his carriage, Philemon says thoughtfully, 'Not many miles south of here lies the city of Troy, Homer's Ilium.'

I catch my breath; in a way I'd always assumed that Troy really had existed. But Homer's 'windy city' was so deeply embedded in my imagination that the boundaries of fantasy and reality had become blurred. Swinging onto Arion, I can see the mighty Achilles wielding his huge spear and flashing shield, taking on Hector to avenge his beloved comrade-in-arms Patroclus.

As our cavalcade winds its way across plains and mountains, verdant valleys and barren deserts, Philemon sometimes asks me to sit in the carriage and read to him. To my delight he's brought with him Xenophon's account of how he led the Ten Thousand back to Greece after their victorious battle and then disastrous defeat, when Cyrus, the would-be new King of Persia, was killed.

Xenophon pioneered hugely creative approaches to rearguard fighting and set new standards of leadership in the way he looked after his men. But I'm more interested in what the great man doesn't write so much about: what was it like on the long march to Cunaxa, where the fatal battle took place? And how close is Cunaxa to Babylon – where we're headed to try and talk to the King of Kings? As we rattle along in the carriage, I'm full of questions. 'Why did Xenophon sign up for this in the first place, sir?'

Philemon glances outside at the cavalryman escorting us. 'Xenophon has always had his own ideas about how to rule; whether democracy, as in Athens, is better than oligarchy – which, despite your two kings, is what you have in Sparta. He felt that Cyrus's rebellion against his brother, the Persian king Artaxerxes II, was justified.'

'And the Greeks proved themselves stronger, didn't they? They were on the verge of taking Babylon. Then Cyrus had to go and get himself killed!'

Philemon's voice is quiet. 'The death of Cyrus was completely unnecessary; appalling judgement on his part in refusing to accept sound advice. And I'm sure that Xenophon thought so too.' He leans towards me as the carriage jolts and rumbles. 'But you see, Lycon, this was always Xenophon's greatest strength. He never let adversity overcome his intense creativity as a leader. Once he was elected general, one of the replacements for those who were tricked and slaughtered by the Persians, his sole mission was to bring his men home.'

I have good reason to remember Philemon's words over the next few weeks. The cavalry riders are far more than just an escort. They frequently send out scouts far ahead, who report back about the safety of the road we're following. They also look to our provisioning: purchasing supplies wherever they are plentiful and the people are friendly. The cavalry commander, Aegeus, regularly reports to Philemon; he reminds me of Leon, he's so strong and intelligent. One evening, warmly welcomed by my master, Aegeus comes and sits by our fire and joins our supper. He looks at Arion and then at Philemon. 'You have a fine animal, sir.'

My master gestures towards me. 'As to that, Lycon is the rider. He can tell you far more about Arion than I can.'

Aegeus turns towards me with a friendly smile. 'He can run, eh, Lycon?'

I smile back, caught up in our joint love of fine horses. 'Your mare looks pretty special, sir. She has Arabian in her, doesn't she?'

'She does. We'll do a race when this is all over! Meanwhile,' he looks at my master, 'we have wolves on our back, sir. We need to discuss how to deal with them.'

This news seems to come as no surprise to my master. 'What do you suggest, Aegeus?'

Aegeus takes a stick and traces lines in the sand around the fire. 'They are coming closer, night by night. We are letting them become more confident by doing nothing. By tomorrow night they are likely to try a raid on the rear of the baggage train. Then, I suggest, is our time to strike.'

Philemon says, 'Shock and awe?'

'Yes, sir. A full charge, no quarter and chase the rest until we kill them too.'

After Aegeus has returned to brief his men, I look at my master. 'That's what Xenophon did, when the Ten Thousand were being harried from behind, wasn't it, sir?'

Philemon gives a last stir to the flames of the fire, as they shoot out a few dying sparks. 'We do well to take our lessons from the master of the rearguard action, Lycon. Xenophon's greatest weapon was deceit, and it must be ours. We fool the enemy into thinking that they have the upper hand. Or that we don't know they are there. Or that we are doing nothing to hinder them – when we are planning the opposite.'

'Does Aegeus know what their numbers are?'

'Not as many as they would like us to think. And the psychological damage of their entire sortie being slaughtered will be a great setback, no matter how many they are.'

As I curl up with Arion's halter rope round my middle and look at the stars blazing in the sky above, I wonder at these amazing Athenian warriors. And I remember that the warrior who is reshaping the Spartan army and navy is an Athenian by birth.

*

Aegeus' hunch was correct. The 'wolves', whosever mercenaries they might have been, were never allowed to get anywhere near the baggage train. I found out afterwards that as the attackers began their charge, the Athenian cavalry burst out of the trees on either side of them with such speed and ferocity that the less disciplined horses of the enemy wheeled in terror and bolted. The 'shock and awe' of the ambush was increased by riders behind the front line bashing their shields with their spears in an ear-numbing racket (another Xenophon tactic). Then, with clinical precision, Aegeus and his riders did what was planned. They left one survivor to run for it, so that he could tell the tale to whoever had sent them. The horses of the dead were left unharmed and turned loose.

*

There comes barren territory where we're very glad that extra provisions have been purchased in places where the people were friendly and food was plenty. Aegeus shows his care for all members of his convoy by making sure that the pack animals have fodder when the ground is too bare for them to forage.

After many days of this desert, we enter a river gorge where the cliffs tower a good three hundred feet above us to our left. On our right runs the river, fast and deep, with more cliffs rising on the other side. Aegeus and his men have scouted this well in advance in case of ambush, and still they ride ahead of the cavalcade on high alert. Even then there is no room on the narrow track for the cavalry to ride more than four abreast. It's a gloomy place, with the mules' hoof-fall echoing towards the crags and the animals themselves unsettled and nervous. We proceed through the gorge for around five miles before the cliff height gradually drops and we arrive in less hostile surroundings.

These lands remind me of a passage in Xenophon's account of the Ten Thousand's march towards Babylon. Excitedly, I read it to Philemon:

> *'Large and beautiful plain country, well-watered and thickly covered with trees of all sorts and vines. Shut in on all sides by a steep and lofty wall of mountains from sea to sea.'*

We get out of the carriage and watch the pack animals drinking deep, standing in the shallow river. Their peaks wreathed in clouds, mountain ranges surround us, and I wonder how we're going to cross them. 'This scenery looks like Xenophon's account of Cilicia, doesn't it, Master?'

'Indeed.'

Before we can get to the mountains, we have the river to cross. It must be nearly two hundred feet wide. Aegeus nudges his horse gently into the water and scouts a route. He waves us on, and his riders take the bridles of the pack animals. Slowly, they guide them into the clear water, so clear, that I can see darting fish swimming beneath. Philemon and I ford the river on foot, as I lead Arion across. It never comes up beyond our waists and we make it easily to the other side.

Two days' march further on, we encounter a river too deep to ford. And where there are signs that someone doesn't want us to cross it by any other means. There were boats moored here to cross in, but they've been burned.

Without needing any order from their leader, the cavalrymen set to work felling young trees. In a matter of hours, they've built two robust rafts. The pack animals are unharnessed from the carts and led into the water. With some gentle persuasion from Aegeus' riders, they start to swim alongside the cavalry horses. The water is swift-running, but the riders hold them firmly and their own horses are powerful swimmers. All make it without mishap to the other side and are tethered to forage. Then the cavalry return, load the carriages and carts onto the rafts, and take them across in relays. Philemon is persuaded to sit in his carriage, which is lashed to the raft, while I decide to find out how much Arion likes to swim with me on board. He splashes into the water and launches himself like he does this every day. Once on the other side, we pitch camp for the night. But I can't help wondering uneasily who burned those boats.

The following day, as our convoy weaves through woodland, we get an answer. Hooded riders suddenly close in on us from all sides, outnumbering our cavalry. I am riding Arion at the time, beside my master's carriage, and I wish heartily that I was armed to help fight off these raiders. But our cavalry fight solidly back and their professionalism as highly trained killers soon starts to fray the ranks of the robber band. Many of our soldiers, having unseated the raiders, have dismounted to finish them off in hand-to-hand combat – among them, their leader Aegeus. Suddenly, one of the bandits decides to make a run for it, but not without some plunder. Seizing the bridle of Aegeus's grey dappled mare, he gallops off towards the mountains. Seething with anger, and knowing that with the battle almost won, my master is safe,

I urge Arion after him. They're galloping fast, but now my midnight charger shows what he is made of. In all my short life on horseback, I have never travelled as swiftly as this.

Within a few minutes we're right behind them, and Arion knows exactly what I'm planning, edging alongside until we're running parallel. Now I know I have to act swiftly or my beloved horse will be in mortal danger from this scoundrel's knife. I throw myself across the narrow gap between us and drag him kicking and flailing to the ground. We tumble together in the dust and I see his fist rise, clutching a dagger. Seizing his wrist, I sit astride him, pin his arm to the ground and punch him hard in the head. He lies still.

His horse and Aegeus's mare have stopped and are nosing around for forage. Arion, I would swear, is standing guard over them, such is the authoritative curve of his neck. With a thunder of hooves, one of Aegeus's men approaches and grins as he sees me dusting myself off next to the motionless robber. 'Aegeus will be your friend for life, young man. He's inordinately fond of this lady.'

I grin back, stroking my dark horse. 'He challenged me to a race – but we know who is the faster animal now!'

He takes the mare's bridle and also the reins of the robber's horse, while I swing back onto Arion. 'We'll leave him to his dreams. He won't get far on foot.'

Back at the convoy, the soldiers are removing the robber horses' saddles and bridles and sending them off to the wild with a slap on the rump. I slide off Arion and Aegeus shakes my hand. 'That was a brave move, taking him on unarmed, young Lycon.'

'I was just worried that he might harm Arion, sir.'

'Who lacks armour too. And, I must concede, has the edge on speed over my sprightly mare.'

When we strike camp that evening, Aegeus eats with my master and me once more. He explains how journeying in this kind of country is similar to sailing in the Aegean – it's just that the pirates are on horseback.

'Are they in the pay of some robber baron?'

'Sometimes. You also get mercenaries who have decided to go it alone.'

Philemon says, 'So the standards of soldiery must vary considerably?'

'This lot were better equipped than the first bunch. And I'm afraid they don't hesitate to fight dirty, too.'

I have to know more, after what I exposed my brave Arion to earlier. 'What do you mean by dirty, sir?'

'They tip their daggers with lethal poison. Something that a Greek soldier would never do.'

For all of that night, I don't sleep. With Arion's lead rope wrapped tightly round my waist, I lie in the grass and listen to his peaceful munching. And I resolve to never ever take him into such terrible danger again.

*

As the road winds ever nearer to the mountains, Philemon draws my attention to a staging post where a horse is tethered inside a barn with water trough, fodder and a guard alongside. 'The courier network of the Persians. If you have to take flight with a message for Athens, I'm sure that your Krypteian cunning will enable you to take advantage of these.'

'I've been noticing them, sir. They're roughly a day's fast ride apart, would you say?'

'Yes. Could be a godsend in desert country.'

Every time one of these staging posts appears, I'm reminded more and more of the vast reach of the Persian Empire. And how its giant shadow could soon be reaching out once more towards Greece.

*

The mountain crossing first involves several days of steep climbing up rutted tracks that seem to jolt the carriages and carts to pieces. The rough terrain causes one of the mules to go lame and there is no choice but to slaughter the poor animal and use its meat. The temperature becomes very cold at night, though remaining hot in the day. My master sleeps in the carriage and I wrap him with animal skins to keep him warm. I feel relieved when the punishing path turns into a gradual descent. Although this in some ways is harder than going upwards because of the slipperiness of the stones. But our brave mules pick their way steadily downhill, while Arion dances lightly beneath me. I breathe a sigh of relief as the path starts to level out. And I gaze in wonder at the terrain before us.

Xenophon describes it.

> *'In this region, the ground was one long level plain, stretching far and wide like the sea… No trees but wild game of all kind – wild asses, ostriches, bustards and antelopes.'*

My master says we are passing over a part of Arabia, which I never expected to have so much wildlife, only ever anticipating barren desert. The cavalry go hunting and stock us up with piles of meat, which I have hardly ever eaten and don't like very much. But you eat what you get. To my relief, they can never catch the ostriches, which are way too fast.

As we draw to the end of this long march, the cavalry ride close around us. We're approaching a city with high walls which rise up like a cliff face ahead. Philemon murmurs, 'Babylon.' So now we are following in Xenophon's footsteps no longer; we have come further than he and his men did. Past Cunaxa, where they fought so hard and so successfully for Cyrus, who wanted to snatch the Persian kingdom from his older brother. Cunaxa, where Cyrus turned victory into defeat by not doing as he'd been strongly advised: entering battle instead of staying at the back. And getting himself killed as a result. Leaving Xenophon to take the Ten Thousand on the most horrifically tough journey of more than three and a half thousand miles back to Greece. Under fierce attack for most of the way.

Along the road to Babylon, there are cohorts of armed guards wearing baggy trousers and plumes on their turbans, and with flashing sabres in their belts. Our cavalry, under the diplomatic command of Aegeus, dismounts to show that we are ambassadors, not invaders. We are allowed to proceed at a walking pace, with armed guards to our front, sides and rear.

As we get closer, the walls rise higher and higher; they must be sixty feet tall. The road we are on leads up to an enormous gate, adorned with vivid blue tiles framed with smaller tiles of gold and turquoise. Amid the blue tiles are images of bulls and dragons. Philemon says quietly, 'The Ishtar Gate: named after the Persians' goddess of love and war.'

'Love and war? That's a strange union, Master.'

'Do not forget, Lycon, that when Aphrodite tired of her loving husband Hephaestos, she had an affair with Ares, god of war.'

I had forgotten; it makes me wonder how love can be in so many ways as dangerous as war. With a heavy heart, I think of the tear-stained face of my little mistress, hugging Xerxes, as she begs me not to leave her.

*

The Persian troops halt us a hundred feet from the Gate of Ishtar. Their leader tells Philemon that we may set up camp here and wait for our audience with the Grand Vizir of the King of Kings. Under a night sky of flashing stars and occasional showers of meteorites, we do as they say. Over our campfire, Philemon gives me a final briefing. 'I do not expect a change of heart. But by approaching them, we are sending a message. That we are all human beings living under the same skies, and we should be able to talk.'

'What kind of result are you looking for, Master?'

'I want them to know that they will not be taking us by surprise.'

'Make them pause for thought?'

'And that could buy us valuable time. That is our code word, Lycon – "time". As soon as I use that word, you must ride on wings to take the warning back to Athens and Sparta.'

'So you're not hoping to stop them invading?'

He smiles his slight smile. 'Of course I hope – but I doubt that we can change anything. However, it is always useful to look our enemy in the face and try to understand them.'

'Leon said something like that: about getting into the enemy's head, to be better able to defeat them.'

'Leon is a wise commander.' Philemon takes the signet ring from the middle finger of his right hand and gives it to me. 'You must take this to Aristides, my most trusted friend, who also is a leader of the assembly. You know where he lives, don't you?'

'Yes, sir.' I tuck the ring well inside my tunic. Climbing into the carriage, wrapped up from the chill of the night with animal skins, Philemon falls into a fitful sleep. I look at his gentle, broad-browed face, thinking how much he reminds me of Xenophon. One, a man of peace and the other a warrior, but remarkably alike.

While we are breakfasting the following morning, my master says, 'Do not accept any offers of food or drink, Lycon. Their aim will be to make us ill and then complain that we have brought the plague as our gift. They may even use it as an excuse to slay us.' We wait on the bidding of the Grand Vizir for the whole day. And for three more long days.

On the fifth day, as evening draws in, a cohort of soldiers in resplendent turbans and trousers approaches our camp. I can see some of our cavalrymen surreptitiously exchanging glances of amusement; compared with their full armour, spears and swords, these showy beings must resemble a gaggle of exotic birds. And gaggle is the right word, for their formation has none of the tight discipline of the Athenian warriors. No wonder our men came so close to taking Babylon before Cyrus scored that fatal own goal.

Their leader comes up to my master and demands that he shows the gifts he has brought. Philemon reaches into the carriage, beneath the seat, and brings out a package wrapped in soft cloth. The leader gestures with his sabre and my master carefully unwraps a glittering gold and jewel-encrusted bridle. There's a murmur of approval from the Persian guard and I admire what a masterstroke this gift is. It acknowledges the Persians as superb horsemen, warriors and conquerors. I wonder who crafted it. Philemon has yet more to offer, and it's just as clever. The second package is unwrapped to reveal a magnificent sabre in the Persian style; its curving blade flashes pure silver and its handle gold and rubies. The symbolic value is huge. Athens is laying down its sword to acknowledge the power of Persia. We come in all humility. Whatever the outcome of this audience, the Persian King will hopefully let us depart unharmed.

The leader of the Grand Vizir's bodyguard signals to my master to accompany them inside the Gate of Ishtar. Carrying the gifts, I am allowed to follow him. The enormous sixty-foot-high gate swings ponderously open to allow us to enter. Then, just as slowly, it closes, leaving our cavalry and baggage train outside.

*

Seated on a golden throne within a hall of soaring height, the Grand Vizir regards my master from behind half-closed eyelids. My gaze downwards, I kneel with the precious gifts.

His head bowed in submission, my master remains silent, waiting for the Grand Vizir to speak. The voice is hoarse, like he maybe shouts a lot. 'What makes you presume that you can expect any reception here other than death, after you executed the ambassadors we sent to you?'

Some backstory here. Actually, those ambassadors were demanding that the whole of Greece must pay tribute to Persia. Quite a few Greek states capitulated, but Athens and Sparta went beyond a cursory 'No, thank you' and murdered the Persian envoys, for which Persia never forgave them. It didn't help that subsequent invasion attempts by Persia failed, despite their vast numerical superiority to the Greek troops. So it could be argued that we brought all this on ourselves. It could be, but I'm arguing no such thing; Greece was not the aggressor. But we should not have killed Persia's envoys.

My master's voice is its usual serene calm as he looks respectfully at the Grand Vizir. 'Your Excellency, Athens and Sparta ruptured all the ancient laws of hospitality when they murdered your ambassadors. It would be perfectly understandable if you chose to deal that fate to us.'

There's a pause before the Grand Vizir's next words. 'But unless you are suicidally inclined, there must be some thought in your heads that persuades you to test our hospitality.'

Philemon bows his head. 'Your Excellency, what Athens and Sparta did to the King of King's ambassadors was barbaric. I do not think that any member of the court of the King of Kings is a barbarian.'

In the silence, I hold my breath. I'm sure His Excellency was not expecting this humility. I'm equally sure that he's suspicious of it.

'So tell us, Athenian barbarian, what you have to offer.'

My master raises his head and looks steadily at the Grand Vizir, whose gold-embroidered robes glitter in the torchlight. 'The hand of friendship, Your Excellency. And the tribute that we previously so foolishly refused to pay.'

'Even if the tribute is increased tenfold?'

'Even so. We will add to it much silver from our mines at Laurium.'

The Grand Vizir whispers to a colleague. Then he turns back to my master. 'You seem very confident, barbarian. What expectations do you have of the outcome of this audience?'

Philemon bows his head again. 'I do not presume to have any expectations, Your Excellency. All I have is hope.'

'Because Athens and Sparta cannot afford another war?'

'I cannot speak for Sparta. But Athens has neither the desire nor the means to prosecute another war. Especially not a war against the King of Kings.'

'Even though the results were as they were, all that time ago?'

'Even so. We cannot rely on the fortunes of war to deal us another favourable hand. We are well aware that when the might of the King of Kings strikes, empires fall.'

The eyes of the Grand Vizir are hooded behind his heavy lids. He says slowly, 'You appreciate that the King of Kings is a busy man. It could be some days before he can respond to you. But I will concede, Athenian barbarian, that your attitude to us is pleasingly different from what we expected.'

'I will wait with our entourage, Your Excellency.'

'We will be happy to offer you and your slave the hospitality that our ambassadors did not receive from you.'

'Your Excellency, I would not dare to presume on such generosity.' We both prostrate ourselves as the Grand Vizir leaves with his retinue. Philemon whispers to me, 'Time is now of the essence.' And there is the word.

SIX

'ARION... A HORSE OF DIVINE RACE'

Homer, The Iliad, Book 23

Four sabre-armed guards escort us back to our little camp outside the walls. They march off, but I have a feeling that they've stationed themselves not far away in the darkness, and there are many more Persian troops around us. Philemon sits in his carriage and is joined there by Aegeus; they converse in low tones. I feel for my master's signet ring in my tunic. Then I lead Arion into the shadows to saddle and bridle him. Those guards and that Grand Vizir and his King of Kings need to think that we're all waiting here like dummies for more news from on high. But we've had all the news we need.

I lead Arion quietly away from the camp until we're engulfed by the night. Before I mount, I stroke his fine neck and murmur a soft greeting. He turns his head to me, nostrils flaring, eager for the run. The night is cool and his hooves will be sure, his legs strong. 'You'll fly this, Beautiful. Just like Pegasus.' Then I swing onto his back and we take off. Galloping on the sand to the side of the road, Arion runs almost silently. I don't think anyone has seen or heard this black horse and his rider disappear. Leaving behind the high walls of Babylon and the blue Gate of Ishtar like fading shadows.

There are plenty of stories about runners who died bringing news to some place or other, and about horses that were galloped into the ground for the sake of being a few hours faster. No news on earth is worth the death of the messenger.

So Arion and I play it fast, but not furious. We're following the route that we came by. Not the dreadful northern path that Xenophon had to fight his way through to get home with the Ten Thousand: across freezing, snow-covered mountains, attacked by hostile tribes, endlessly harried by Artaxerxes' armies. The route that Arion and I are following is used by Persian couriers, with staging points a day's gallop apart. There, horses are changed over and new steeds depart. As Philemon suggested, with my Krypteian training, we can take advantage of that.

Galloping onwards through the night, I try and judge when I should ease the pace. I listen to Arion's breathing as those flaring nostrils fill the deep chest with air. It's regular and even; he's hit a rhythm, with that mighty heart a steady drumbeat. When I sit back to slow him a little, he ignores me completely. In the end I have to admit that he's in charge of this ride, not me. So, like I did with Balios on the mountain assault course, I give my flying horse his head.

Hours later, as dawn casts its first thin strands of light across the horizon, Arion slows to a canter then a walk and takes a turn off the road, down a sloping bank. Ahead of us, I can hear the murmur of water. He probably scented it miles ago. I slide off his back and unsaddle him, and he wades into the stream, dipping his nose to drink. I join him. Then he rolls on the grassy bank and starts to graze. I rummage in my saddle bag for the morsels of bread and fruit I've been saving from our meals. And all the time, I'm listening out for the sound of hooves on the road.

I must have dozed off, when I'm wakened by Arion giving me a gentle nudge in the ribs with his nose. The sun is well clear of the horizon. Looking back down the road, can I see a cloud of dust? Or is it heat shimmer? Quickly I saddle up and we're on our way. The heat intensifies, but so does our speed. My Arabian is doing what he was born to, with brothers and sisters who know no other life than the desert and its endless stretches between watering holes.

We get to a staging post and gallop straight past it. If a rider is after us, he'll have to change horses here. And for miles previously, his mount must have been tiring. As we flash past, I glance behind to see the guard looking in our direction. So when our pursuer arrives there, he'll have an informant. I start to make a battle plan, with my master's words echoing in my head:

Xenophon's greatest weapon was deceit, and it must be ours.

When we reach the next staging post, it's cool night and Selene's gentle light glints on the dusty road. This time,

Arion is happy to take a break from galloping and forage among some trees, while I keep watch. After an hour or so, a rider approaches on a lathered horse. He leads it into the barn. I creep closer to try and catch any conversation between him and the guard. It may be that it's not us he's pursuing at all, but it would be very useful to know.

I can't hear what they're saying, and soon after the man rides out on a fresh animal. Inside the barn, the exhausted horse is being watered, fed and rested before its next all-day galloping stint. And the guard could now be keeping an eye out for us; it's time to leave. Without even a tail swish, as though Arion is well aware how important quietness is, we slip away into the night. But it's good to know that our pursuer, if that's what he turns out to be, is now in front of us, thinking that we're ahead of him.

Our most important goal now is not to go too fast because we don't want to catch up with the rider. But Arion is now stopping more frequently to drink, each time he scents a stream, his desert instincts driving him to make the most of water when he finds it.

Hints of dawn are tinting the horizon when we come to the next staging post. There's very little cover, so we have to watch from a distance; it could be that the rider is about to depart on a fresh horse, or that he has already gone. Then, I see the guard leading a horse out of the barn, accompanied by the rider. There's a discussion going on, as the guard leads the horse in a circle and the rider gesticulates. Now I can see what this is all about. The animal has a slight limp. They go back into the barn. Stealthily, my dark horse and I pass by behind the building before rejoining the road half a mile on.

We're ahead again – and unless there's a spare horse in that barn, we're going to open up a big gap between the hunter and the hunted. Between dawn and midday, Arion's flying hooves devour the miles, before we take another break. We're on the plain where the cavalry went after all the animals. A few wild asses are grazing in the distance as I dismount and set about filling my saddlebags with fodder; that barren mountain range is looming and we'll need to bring our own food to get through it. As though he knows what's ahead, Arion chomps grass for a good long time.

The mountain crossing is the toughest part of the ride because of the cold. I can see that Arion hates it too. So we don't stop; we just keep moving, day and night. Sometimes I dismount and feed Arion snacks of fodder as I walk beside him; a walk is all we can do, up those stony slopes and finally down the other side.

By the time we've put the mountains behind us, we're both exhausted and very hungry. As the staging post that I first noticed on our journey to Babylon comes into view, I know that I have to do something about this. Dismounting, I let Arion forage for what he can find among some spindly trees. For a long time, I watch the building for any sign of activity. Then I start to edge towards it, ready to flatten myself on the ground if anyone suddenly appears. But it's eerily silent, with no riders approaching and no one coming outside. As I reach the barn and peer round the entrance, I can see that it's deserted. No horses and no guard. But no sign of a struggle.

Then I spot what I'm looking for: a hay net full of fodder and a drinking trough. I go outside and call Arion. He approaches warily; I stroke him to reassure him and show him the food and water. While he eats and drinks, I do some further rummaging and find half a loaf that's been abandoned as casually as everything else. Then I keep watch outside in case whoever was here decides to return. When we move on, I take all the remaining hay in the net with me on my back.

Arriving at the river where the boats were burned, I wonder if whoever destroyed them is responsible for the deserted staging post. If someone is still following us, he's going to find cold comfort in that empty barn when he arrives with his shattered horse.

Holding the hay net above my head to keep the fodder dry, I keep a sharp lookout as Arion swims us across; a river crossing is the classic place for an ambush, as Xenophon points out. Emerging from the water unscathed and quickly putting many miles behind us, we have no need of the hay as we cross the verdant countryside of Cilicia. But heading again into the barren landscape that will take us in a few more days to the coast, I am very grateful that I can feed my valiant Arion. As for me, it's a while since I ran out of bread crusts, and I wish that I could eat hay.

We're under a blazing sun, dust rising from Arion's hooves, when something makes me look behind us. A cloud is on the horizon; it takes me some time to work out that it's a dust cloud. Someone is after us. It may be whoever burned the boats. Or just some more robber bands, like those who attacked us on the way to Babylon. But even my black Arabian must be getting tired by now; can we hide somewhere? I look around and see only desert dunes. That's when Arion takes over from his hesitant rider. He can probably smell the enemy from here. With a snort and a toss of the head, he leaps into a gallop. And keeps galloping, hour after hour, until there is no more sign of the dust cloud. Even then, he doesn't stop, ignoring my attempts to slow him.

That's when I begin to understand what the Arabian horse is. To the desert riders who depend utterly on him, he must be a god. All-powerful, all-seeing and all-knowing. With a massive generosity and the greatest heart. I have no doubt that Arion saved my life on more than one occasion on that ride. And he must have pushed himself to his very limit in going without water and food. I can never think about my horse of divine race without awe.

*

As Arion and I crest the cliff and look down on the sea and those Athenian triremes, I remember Xenophon's account of the ecstatic cries of his men as they gazed at the ocean and knew they had escaped the Persians. Not this ocean, but our emotions cannot be that different, looking at the blue horizon. 'The sea! The sea!' they cried. And my heart is singing out too. Arion is his usual majestic, quiet self. But he needs no nudge from me to start delicately descending the cliff path.

We've been spotted by keen eyes as soon as we appeared on the cliff. Antilochus climbs up with a cohort of men to escort us to the ships. He frowns. 'By Zeus, lad, you're skin and bone!'

'I wasn't the one who had to do the work.'

'Maybe, but your time for Hades is not yet. You still have a mission to fulfil!'

'Have you got plenty of water for Arion? He's very thirsty!'

'Plenty of water. And food that you must eat, Wolf Cub!'

On the voyage back to Greece, I just eat and sleep. When I'm not doing that, I'm making sure that Arion is drinking and eating his fill, because his ribs were starting to show on the final days of that desert trek. Antilochus has provided some good fodder for Arion, and abundant supplies of cheese, figs and watered wine for me. When I doze off for the third time, there are storm clouds building on the horizon. My dreams are all about galloping across endless mountains. When I wake up, I'm lying beside Arion and find I've slept right through the gales, while the ship pitched and rolled.

Antilochus smiles. 'Your sensible animal lay down in his straw. We put you in there with him.'

Arion is looking well rested and bright as I lead him down the gangplanks in the harbour. Antilochus is already ordering his men to ready the ship for the voyage back, to wait for Philemon and his retinue. But he turns as I approach with the black stallion. 'I am so very grateful to you, Antilochus.'

He grasps my hand in a grip that reminds me of Pyro. 'Looks like Athens could be very grateful to you, Lycon. May the goddess be with you!'

They've given me a sackful of forage plus bread and fruit for me, and it's not going to be difficult to find water in the friendlier lands we're riding now. But it comes as a shock on the night when I realise that we're trotting into Athens' dark, smelly streets. I find it hard to ride past my master's house, wondering if my little mistress Lydia is there and whether I'll ever see her again. Hoping that she'll soon forget Lycon the slave. With that familiar ache in my heart, I ride on to the impressive villa where Philemon's trusted friend Aristides lives.

He's expecting me. His groom takes Arion, while the master of the house ushers me into an inner room where slaves don't normally get received. I give him the signet ring. 'My master says the Persian King is definitely preparing for war, sir.'

'Sit down, Lycon. Philemon has told me of his plans to make you a free man, because of the service you are rendering to Athens. So we meet now as citizens, not master and slave.' He orders food and water, and I recount the audience with the Grand Vizir pretty well word for word. Aristides smiles grimly when I come to the bit about Athens offering to pay tribute. 'That was clever of Philemon. He knew that if the offer of such wealth did not elicit even a blink of interest, then Persia's mind was already made up. Now, do you have any idea, Lycon, when he might get back to Athens?'

'If the Persians leave him alone, he'll be maybe three weeks behind me, sir.'

'You have done well. First thing tomorrow, the assembly will know of this and decisions must be taken.'

I hesitate to ask in case it seems out of order, but I have to know: 'Sir, do you think that Athens will ask Sparta for help to fight the Persians?'

A shadow crosses his fine features. 'Thebes and Corinth, very possibly. But Sparta… why do you ask, young Lycon?'

'It's just that I was tutoring history with the little mistress Lydia, and we were looking at the forming of allies… that's all.'

Aristides claps his hands for a slave to attend us. 'We would do well to learn from history, Lycon. Sparta is not to be trusted as an ally.'

A very pretty slave girl shows me to my bed in the hayloft and admires Arion before wishing me goodnight. The Arabian has been well looked after. He has plenty of water and a bed of straw which he's lying on, looking very contented. I sit down next to him for a while and hug him and stroke his fine mane. Then I whisper, 'Time to move on, my friend?'

He's on his feet before I can take a breath. Minutes later, my horse of the gods saddled and bridled, we're making our way down Athens' dark streets towards the road that will take us to Sparta.

*

I'm hoping that Aristides will assume that I've gone back to Philemon's house in the early hours of the morning, taking Arion with me, in order to not be any more trouble to him. After all, he has his own business with the assembly now. And his views on Philemon's freeing me might not be quite the same as those of my former master. As Arion and I fly down the narrow neck of land that connects Athens with Sparta, I'm heartily glad to be a free man again. But

I'll always remember Philemon's kindness. And I can never think of my little mistress without an aching heart, her sweet singing echoing in my head.

We're barely ten miles from Sparta when I become aware that we have company. The terrain is rocky, so we can't use speed to put a distance between us and our pursuers. And it's only at night. Like a glimpse of someone flitting between rocks. Sometimes a faint murmur of voices. Other times, the distant glimmer of a fire on the mountain. Looks like the helots are becoming more organised. Or is it someone else?

From that point, Arion and I are on permanent full alert. We keep moving, with me walking beside him over the rougher mountain tracks. And all the time, the hairs on the back of my neck are bristling. Arion can sense our shadowers better than me; sometimes he stops, sniffs the air and rumbles a low whinny. It reminds me of that night more than two years ago when Zena and I took the stillborn lamb up Mount Taygetos to lure the wolf away from our sheep. And all the time, the wolf was just above us. But he, I am sure, meant us no harm. Whereas these men will want to rob and kill me and steal my horse of the gods.

But the long journey has taken its toll. Both of us are tired and yearning to be at our destination. I stroke Arion's strong neck. 'Not far now, Beautiful.' All the same, I sometimes think that we're both of us almost sleepwalking along these mountain tracks. Idly, I wonder if the Krypteia know about who is shadowing us. If not, I'll have to tell Leon when we get back. If we get back… the more tired you become, the more pessimistic you are. I try to shake myself out of it; we are so close to Sparta now. And I can't wait for Zena to see Arion.

Night is about to give way to dawn. Selene has hidden her face, shrouded in gloomy cloud. We've almost quit the mountain paths and under the stars we're looking out over the plains that will lead to Sparta. I'm about to fling myself onto Arion's back, when it's not a wolf that pounces but a rock that whistles past my ear. Instinctively I let go of Arion's reins and shout, 'Run, Beautiful!' Then something hits the back of my head so hard that dark takes me.

It takes me beneath the earth. I'm walking through shadowy caverns alongside a swirling black underground river. And I'm not alone. Walking beside me is a warrior. I can't see his face because of the golden helmet with its fierce horsehair cockade. Inside the muscled breastplate moves a powerful form. Yet I hear no sound from the warrior's armour, nor from the turbulent river.

After what seems like an eternity of walking, the warrior positions himself in front of me, sword raised to block my path. Looking at the darkness behind the eyeholes of the helmet towering above me, it's like when Zena and I first met Leon that night on the mountain. In terror at that darkness, I lower my head. And shafts of light pierce my eyes.

As I wake up, my head is thumping like it's being kicked by a mule, and the backs of my legs are rubbing on something hard. My head's been bandaged and I'm being carried on a shield, like that poor devil they brought into the forge for Pyro to fix. But it's two Krypteian soldiers who are marching with this shield. Struggling to a sitting position,

I look around and see Leon leading Arion beside me. In front and behind are his Krypteian troops. We're crossing the plain that will take us to Sparta. His blue eyes fixing mine in a steady gaze, Leon says, 'Welcome back from the River Styx, Wolf Eyes.'

As dark dream and bright daylight blur, I mumble, 'I gave your regards to Achilles.'

'What did he have to say?'

'Same as he said to Odysseus: he'd rather be the most wretched slave alive on earth than a prince among the dead.'

'You don't look like the happiest slave I've ever seen – how's your head?'

'Sore. Can I have my horse back, please?'

The stretcher bearers halt and I swing stiffly off the shield. Leon strokes Arion's neck. 'He won't let me near his back!'

With creaking muscles and a splitting head, I swing on board my black beauty. 'He's careful about strangers.'

'You need to be more so.'

Our march resumes. 'I thought we'd made it out of the mountains… glad you were there.'

'So am I. I wondered if you were leaving us.'

'So did I.'

Leon's voice becomes businesslike. 'Now – what news do you bring, Wolf Eyes?'

SEVEN

TAKING THE FIGHT TO THE ENEMY

For a while after I've explained where the real threat to Sparta lies, Leon says nothing. He looks at me in surprise when I tell him of Philemon's wish to join forces with Sparta, and the opposition he's facing from his countrymen. Then I explain how Philemon is an old friend of Xenophon. At this point, Leon sharpens the pace to a jog. 'No time to lose!'

'That was Philemon's code word to send me on my way.'

It's midday when we arrive at Danae's estate. The stallions in the paddocks call to Arion and he gives a throaty response. Zena comes running out and exclaims when she sees the Arabian. I slide off him. 'He'll appreciate a drink!'

'I'll look after him myself – what's he called?'

When I tell her, she says, 'Perfect! Come on, Arion!' Without looking once at my bloody, bandaged head, she leads the way to the stables. And after spending the last three thousand miles with his fellow traveller, Arion happily follows her without a backwards glance. Despite my headache, I can't help laughing and Leon suppresses a smile.

The Krypteia have melted away as Danae comes out of the villa to greet us. She looks shocked to see me and I feel awkward to appear so ragged in front of such a beautiful woman. 'Lycon, you're pitifully thin! Come inside and let me see to your head!' Half an hour later, bathed, clothed in a new tunic and with my head wound cleaned up, I feel as though I have at last rejoined the land of the living. Although the memory of that dark underground river and the stern warrior will never leave me.

As Leon and I follow Danae and Zena into the dining room, I'm nervous at the thought of meeting the great man again. But Xenophon welcomes me as if I were his own son; his arms go round me in a bear hug that takes my breath away. With the food lying untouched before us, I deliver my message in suitably Laconic style. Then Danae says firmly, 'Now this young man must be allowed to eat!'

And eat we all do, before anyone else speaks, except to compliment our gracious hostess on the food. I catch Zena's eye from time to time, and she still has that secret smile for me. She approves, and that's more than enough.

With the plates cleared away, and Danae and Zena gone to thoroughly check over Arion, Xenophon says, 'You tell us, Lycon, that my old friend Philemon is a member of the Athens assembly?'

'Yes, sir. And still your great friend.'

'And he wishes that Sparta could join Athens in defending ourselves against the Persians?'

'Yes, sir. He bade me ride on to Sparta after I had warned Athens, to deliver his message to you.'

Xenophon murmurs, 'I had not expected such an ally.' He looks at Leon. 'How quickly can we convene a meeting of the ephors?'

'I report to them weekly on the movements of the Krypteia.'

'Good. But we must have a rock-solid plan to put before them.'

'I think they will be in favour of a joint defence, sir. But they will want it to be led by Sparta.'

Xenophon's broad brow creases in a frown. 'So not a joint effort at all.'

Leon casually re-positions a couple of knives that have been left on the table. 'I think you can bring them round, sir. Do I take it that your strategy would be that attack is the best form of defence?'

'Most definitely.'

'In which case, co-operation between our two powers will be nothing short of essential if we are going to employ your fine art of deception, sir.' Leon looks at me. 'As I'm sure you can recall from your reading, Lycon?'

Eager to play my part, I plunge in, quoting from Xenophon's Cavalry Commander:

> *'For those near the sea two effective ruses are, to strike*
> *on land while fitting out ships, and to attack by sea while*
> *ostensibly planning a land attack.'*

He smiles. 'You have me word for word, young Lycon. And I see where you are leading, Leon. Each of our forces has its relative strengths. We have not yet the naval power to match the Athenians. While I like to think that Sparta's cavalry is becoming a force to be reckoned with.'

'So it would be a co-operation based on mutual respect for each other's strengths, sir. I also believe that the Krypteia can play a key role in the gathering of intelligence.'

I think back to the start of the expedition to the court of the King of Kings. 'Philemon took pigeons with him to Persia…'

'The Athenians are more advanced than we are with winged messengers. Sparta has some catching up to do there, too.'

Leon says, 'With your agreement, sir, I would like to form a mounted detachment of the Krypteia specifically for intelligence gathering and deploy them to Persia as soon as possible. With pigeons!'

'Would you need to put it before the ephors?'

'I should – but I would rather justify it after the event, when we see what information my crack troops can send us.'

I am hesitating to speak, but speak I must. Xenophon sees me. 'Go on, Lycon.'

'Can't we form some kind of early strike force and start to hit the Persians hard before they are anywhere near us?'

Xenophon says, 'Strike at their rear?'

'Strike anywhere it'll hurt them! You invented these tactics, Master!'

The two men are silent for a few seconds. Then Xenophon says, 'You are right, Lycon. The only way is to take the fight to the enemy: to harry them relentlessly.'

Leon looks at me. 'What are you proposing, Lycon?'

'While your Krypteian intelligence unit is establishing

how far advanced the Persians are with their war preparations, we put together a highly mobile strike force of cavalry and chariots with bowmen. As soon as we know where the Persian army is, we launch our land force. We will also need a spy force of warships to patrol all possible approaches that the Persian navy could make.'

'Without waiting for all the deliberations between Athens and Sparta – that could take months, while the Persians could be on the march.'

'Exactly, Leon. Once a joint battle plan is in place, of course we let all parties know what we're doing. But we can't wait for all the hot air!'

Leon exchanges glances with Xenophon. The older man turns to me. 'It makes sound sense that you and Leon form this strike force while I talk with the ephors and they talk with Sparta's kings. Then the ephors, as Sparta's ambassadors, talk to Athens. You are right; this whole process could become very drawn out and we cannot afford to wait.'

Leon looks closely at Xenophon. 'Am I correct, sir? You are giving Lycon and me permission to form Sparta's intelligence and early strike forces against the Persians?'

He smiles grimly. 'I shall let the ephors know that preparations are already underway to defend Sparta. They can hardly object to that!'

*

Danae insists that I stay at her house until, as she puts it, 'you've regained the muscle to cover those bones'. Makes me feel like one of her horses, but Leon is strongly in agreement.

Before he heads off to his barracks, he says, 'There'll be pigeons sent over tomorrow – their homing training needs to begin immediately.'

I look at Zena and she laughs. 'Don't worry Lycon – I know what we have to do.' As she's used the word 'we', I start to look forward to this pigeon training.

Two large baskets containing fifty bright-eyed pigeons arrive by wagon the next day. We've prepared a spacious, comfortable pigeon loft, and Zena says we need to feed them twice a day. She shows me how to hold a pigeon so that it feels secure and can't start to flap. The next morning, with the pigeons taken out of their loft and put in the baskets, we ride out, leading the wagon. Zena is riding Arion and exclaiming ecstatically over his floating paces. I have my old friend Balios, who seems pleased to see me.

The sun is high when Zena steers the pigeon wagon to the side of the road. 'We're about five miles away from their loft; this'll do to begin with.' She lifts the lid on the first basket, and a cloud of beating wings lifts off into the sky. I lift the lid on the remaining basket and another twenty-five birds soar into the blue. Zena swings back onto Arion. 'Now let's get back and make sure they've got plenty of food to reward them.'

By the time the wagon rumbles up the driveway, most of our feathered travellers have found their way home. Zena insists on a pigeon count and this is nothing like as easy as counting sheep, as the birds just won't stay still. Eventually, we work out that seven pigeons are missing. Just as we're leaving the barn, two stragglers turn up. 'So just five down now,' says Zena. 'We'll come back later and do a recount in case any others make it.' I'm about to comment on how much I'm looking forward to this but think better of it.

Over the next three weeks, Zena and I increase the distances back to the pigeon loft, and each time, the majority of the birds make it home. Some pigeons take a lot longer than others to find their way, and a few don't make it at all. Zena says this is to be expected.

Then one evening, two men from the newly formed mounted detachment of the Krypteia come riding onto the estate with Leon. The men load the pigeon baskets onto the wagon and depart. On board Xanthos, Leon watches them go.

I feel a bit concerned about the birds' lack of experience. 'They'll be flying far greater distances than we've been able to take them.'

Zena says, 'The main thing is, we've embedded in them the knowledge that, wherever they're released, they come back here. Here is where they know they can find food, water and safety.'

'It's still an awfully long way from Persia!'

'Of course, they won't all make it. That's why they'll be released in large flocks, each one carrying the same message from the Krypteia.'

'How are they going to find their way over all that distance?'

'It's a special homing instinct that pigeons have. Anyway, you found your way back from Babylon, didn't you?'

'That was more Arion than me!'

Danae comes out as the pigeon convoy disappears down the driveway. 'I hope you will stay to eat with us, Leon?'

He bows graciously. 'If it will help this wolf cub regain more muscle, gladly, Lady Danae.'

Zena says teasingly, 'Careful, Leon. You don't want to get fat! What would your men say?'

He replies with mock gravity, 'It would be unspeakable in the company of ladies, Zena.' Over dinner, Leon asks me, 'Do you think Philemon will have arrived back in Athens yet?'

'It's four weeks since I delivered his message to Aristides. If his journey has been without incident, I reckon he'll be back.'

'Good. Because Xenophon has had a productive conversation with the ephors. They're all five strongly in favour of an alliance to fight the Persians.'

'Suppose the kings don't agree?'

Danae comments, 'In Sparta, the kings are little more than generals. Provided that the ephors have a majority vote, the kings have to do what they're told. But since the ephors are elected annually and cannot be re-elected, there is a reasonable balance of power.'

Leon adds, 'The ephors also handle all matters to do with foreign relations, so they will be our ambassadors to Athens, as Xenophon explained.'

'So… they're the real rulers, then?'

'From being presidents of the assembly to justices of the supreme court. They also control the Krypteia and the composition of the army.'

'So that's why you report to the ephors on the Krypteia. But the kings – or one of them – lead us into battle?'

'On military expeditions, two ephors will go along to ensure that the king behaves himself. If he doesn't, they can put him on trial and even depose him.'

'What kinds of misbehaviour can you get from a king?'

Danae replies, 'One king, who shall remain nameless, accepted a bribe from the enemy to throw the battle.'

I think back to that time in the forge when I overheard what sounded like a conspiracy to kill a king. Leon sees me frowning. 'Out with it, Wolf Eyes.'

'That cavalryman, Hipparchos – why would he plot regicide?'

'Ah, that…'

'Was it one king plotting against the other?'

'It wasn't as simple as that. Sometimes if a king turns out to be a mischief maker, it's best to keep him exactly where he is but make it clear that he's under observation.'

Zena grins. 'A smack on the wrist?'

'Not for Hipparchos. He was exiled.'

'That's why he never came back for his breastplate, then.'

Leon says, 'The ephors have their doubts about both of Sparta's kings. The one we suspect of the plot is entirely untrustworthy and can never be allowed to lead a Spartan army. While the king who would take us into battle has integrity but lacks judgement in military affairs.'

Danae suggests, 'And so will be tightly reined in?'

'Indeed, my lady.'

That night, after supper, I thank Danae gratefully for her hospitality and explain that I need to return to the forge to push forward the arming of our cavalry and charioteers. She smiles, 'Of course. But you and Leon must treat this place as your headquarters, and keep sending your charioteers to us for training!'

On the way back, Leon says, 'Come and sleep in the barracks tonight. Contrary to popular belief, the men are given three meals a day, which I would wager is more than you were getting at the forge.' The next morning, insisting that we both wear our crimson tunics and cloaks, he rides with me to look at the progress with chariot manufacture. Pyro is supervising, and he looks like he's enjoying a new lease of life; he's so proud of the mighty chariots with their gleaming bronze panels that the forges are churning out. They're making the harnesses too, replicating the special bridle that Xenophon designed to get the horses' hind legs beneath them.

A thought strikes me as I admire our armourers' handiwork. 'We're going to need a huge supply of high-quality horses for all these chariots.'

'And there,' says Leon, 'we have a tremendous benefactor in the Lady Danae. She has taken it on herself to furnish us with the very finest Thessalian stallions and is training them with Zena.'

'Makes me think of something Xenophon wrote… only the Lady Danae is the opposite.'

He says eagerly, 'Let me… "The rich who don't know how to use their wealth are incurably poor of spirit!" That was your thought, wasn't it?'

'She is a lady very rich of spirit.'

'Her husband was a general who was highly respected by Xenophon and loved by his men; he always put their welfare first and never led them recklessly against an enemy.'

'How did he die?'

Leon's face is like stone as he utters the single word, 'Treachery.'

I'm silent, reflecting on how the bravest of leaders can be undone by an act which they would never think of committing themselves. Leon brightens as we return to our horses. 'Come and see what Xenophon is doing with your chariots, Wolf Eyes!'

On the lower slopes of Mount Taygetos and on the plains beneath, a mock battle is underway. I watch as my chariots thunder down precipitous slopes with their large, iron-clad wheels. Once on the plain, the bowmen unleash storms of arrows. Then the cavalry comes out of nowhere and joins them on either side in a flanking movement, and a deadly charge thunders in a wide arc towards the pretend enemy.

Leon comments, 'The Persians won't like that.'

'Any more than they'll like being attacked from their rear. Or when they think it's all over for the night. Or when they're eating. We need to break all the rules of war as it's normally fought!'

As the cavalry and chariots line up for inspection before Xenophon on his white charger, Leon says, 'The master very much likes your proposal for an early strike force, Wolf Eyes. These are the elite troops he has selected from his training exercises.'

I'm stunned and humbled that Xenophon has personally taken charge of this impulsive plan of mine. 'Who is going to lead them?'

'We are. The master approves of the way we work together.' From the man on the white charger, there is the slightest hint of a nod in our direction. 'Come on!' Leon nudges Xanthos forward and I follow, now at a complete loss for words. We bring our horses to a halt either side of Xenophon's snow-white stallion, who is standing as still as a statue. As Xenophon addresses the troops, the sun clears the horizon and flashes on the bronze helmets with their fierce horsehair crests. Its rays glance off the golden plumage of two eagles circling overhead.

'Warriors of Sparta,' begins the master, 'you have done well in your training and not spared yourselves. You are fully worthy of your election to Sparta's elite early strike force – the first of our men to grasp with an iron glove the throats of those who would make us eat dust.' He pauses, and in the silence comes the sound high above of the two eagles calling to each other. 'I give you your leaders. Leon, who has long been our trusted general of the Krypteia. And Lycon, who has given you a war machine to break the Persians!'

Spartans are normally the deadly, silent types. But at Xenophon's words, a roar goes up and flashing swords rise to the skies.

*

Two days later, Leon and I are riding down the cliff path to the concealed cove which has been turned into Sparta's warship manufacturing base. Through daylight and torchlight, an army of shipbuilders bends, cuts and hammers the oak for the outer hull. The lighter softwoods such as pine, fir and cypress used for the interior make these mighty galleys highly manoeuvrable. Oars are made from a single young fir tree and measure some fifteen feet in length. Wooden pegs and dowels hold the planks of the hull together loosely at first. When a ship is first launched, the wood absorbs water, expanding the hull and making it watertight. At which point a lethal, one hundred and twenty foot-long fighting machine with a ten-foot ram is ready for action. Lined up along the shore, we can see many new triremes awaiting orders; Sparta's shipbuilding operations must soon be a rival for Athens'.

Overseeing operations is Damon, the Krypteian commander of the trireme that took me to Piraeus port for my spying mission. I've come to ask him some very specific questions that are based on a hunch. He shakes hands with me and gives a respectful greeting to his leader. During the ensuing conversation, he continues to keep a close eye on the shipbuilders, occasionally shouting an order.

I start by referring to the pirates who pose such a threat to merchant shipping. 'You told me, I think, Damon, that this sort of thing happens practically every day?'

'It's very common.'

'Do you always pursue any pirate ships that make a run for it? Like you did with the two that went for us?'

'Always. No quarter.'

'How far out might that take you? The Cyclades, maybe?'

'It has happened. We never let them go.'

'And these pirates harry Athenian shipping just as much as our own. So, are there times when Spartan and Athenian warships are chasing the same pirate ships?'

Leon says quickly, 'You can be completely open with us, Damon. We're hoping for a yes.'

A smile passes over Damon's dark-tanned face. 'You have it, Commander.'

Leon continues, 'We appreciate that the laws of the sea make it perfectly natural for Spartans and Athenians to join forces when threatened by a common foe. Now, my comrade will explain in confidence how valuable this informal alliance will be to both our countries.'

I give Damon a brief summary of how we are all threatened by a greater common foe than ever before. A foe which could make its approach by both land and sea. 'It's a tremendous advantage that you and Athens are already co-operating.' I pause and decide to chance another hunch. 'On my spying mission to Athens, I had the opportunity to meet with an Athenian naval commander who impressed me greatly. His name is Antilochus.'

Damon says without hesitating, 'I know him well. We have sunk many pirate ships together.' He looks at Leon. 'Do you wish me to forewarn him of the threat so that we can put in place regular patrols of the islands, Commander?'

'That,' says Leon, 'is exactly what we would like you to do. There will be so much of what my comrade here calls "hot air" before our two countries can join in a formal alliance, that precious time will be lost if we do not act immediately.'

'Immediately it shall be, Commander,' says Damon.

Riding back up the cliff path, we pause to look down on the trireme factory below. Leon says, 'It would seem that Poseidon is onside with both Athens and Sparta for once.'

Three weeks later, after twenty-two more chariots and fifteen more triremes have been built, Arion is seen galloping up to our barracks with Zena on board. She's treasuring a battered-looking pigeon to her chest. 'We had to give her something to eat and drink first, poor thing!'

Leon reaches out and gently takes the exhausted bird from her. His quick fingers unwrap the coded message from the Krypteian mounted troops; the secret service that has penetrated far into Persia to find out what the King of Kings is doing. Handing the pigeon to me, he reads while I try to calm the tired bird. 'The Persian army is in Cilicia. They are three hundred thousand strong.'

Dawn the next day sees a frenzy of activity in Sparta's secret shipyard. Last-minute sea trials are being carried out on the most recently completed warships. Wagon-loads of supplies are being loaded on board the rows of waiting triremes. On the specially adapted boats, chariots are being hauled up the gangplanks, and warhorses cajoled with waiting fodder. Few words need to be exchanged and few orders given, as these crack troops know exactly what needs to be done. They remind me of Aegeus's men; and my heart thuds with excitement at the thought of soon being brothers-in-arms with the Athenians in this fight.

Watching on the clifftop are a jet-black and a snow-white stallion, motionless like their riders, Danae and Xenophon. And now Leon and I are aboard the lead ship in the centre of the fleet, with its fierce eagle heads painted on the prow. Damon is admiral, calling orders for the fleet to line up before hoisting sail. Leon and I raise our swords and the roar goes up with the watchword that Xenophon has set, as the men salute him: 'Zeus Saviour, Heracles Leader!' Xenophon raises his sword in a return salute. Sails are hoisted and our warships swing through the wind, putting the south-westerly behind that will waft us through the islands of the Aegean towards Troy, our landfall.

*

It takes seven days and nights to sail to Troy. The wind is fair and we only encounter one serious storm. Fortunately, when the weather breaks, an island with a sheltering cove is nearby so the fleet can take cover. Any pirates would have had the sense to make a rapid departure if they saw us coming.

Twenty-four hours later, our fleet is beaching on shores where Achilles and his Myrmidons set foot so long ago. In the distance rise the walls of Troy, Troy as it has weathered the many years since Homer's Ilium. Leon says, 'The governor is an Athenian, Menelaos, son of Arrabaios, who expelled a Euboean mercenary leader and was honoured by the Ileans for being such a good friend to them. But we will not be trading on his goodwill, as nothing has yet been formalised between Athens and Sparta.'

Leaving a small cohort in charge of the ships, our task force quickly makes its way up the shore and into the plains towards the mountains. And now we have one major objective: to link up with the Krypteia who have tracked down the foe. And combine our might and stealth to wreak havoc with those who would bring Greece low. The thought of the Grand Vizir's curling lip and hooded eyes makes me boil with anger.

Riding next to me on Xanthos through a star-filled night, Leon says, 'Spit it out, Wolf Eyes.'

I growl, 'Just can't wait to engage with those babies in baggy trousers, that's all!'

He laughs. 'Is that what they wear, these Persian soldiers?'

'Plus, they couldn't hit a dead sheep from three paces. It's just their numbers they rely on.'

Leon says, 'Numbers aren't always on their side – as they've found out before.'

'What they haven't found out yet is what it's like to be attacked in their own territory.'

'I think we'll put the fear of the gods into them, Wolf Eyes.' And that remark of Leon's gets the Hephaestos in me thinking.

*

Five days into the trail, the sun is setting as we climb a mountain track, cavalry and chariots rumbling behind, when Leon raises his hand for a halt. Above us rise harsh red crags, seeming to flame in the light of the low sun. Below, a river plain is opening out. Leon gives a low call, like a bird. And above us, like a horde of ghosts on those red cliffs, rise the Krypteia. Predictably, we haven't found them; they've found us. Their leader, Erebos, tells us that the Persians are camped on the plain for the night, just two miles away.

For several hours, we follow a circuitous route through the mountains, Erebos and his men leading us steadily onwards. Selene is favouring us, just peeping out from trailing cloud once in a while. It's still dark night when we crest a ridge and see below a vast ocean of twinkling lights across the plain.

I whisper to Erebos, 'The officers are in tents, aren't they?'

'Oh, yes – they like their creature comforts.'

Leon says, 'I get your drift, Wolf Eyes. We're going to torch those tents.'

'More than that! We're going to let loose their animals. Capture their provisions. Send them running into the night!'

Minutes later, every bowman who charges down the mountain in those sturdy chariots is shooting arrows of fire. Soon, the plain is alight with burning tents. The cavalry swoop on the provisioning carts and ride off with them. Leon and I slash loose the tethers on the horses and mules and hurry them off into the night, capturing some of the finer animals. The entire attack takes so little time, the Persians have no idea what has hit them. We're gone before they can raise a single sword or shoot one arrow. Melting back into the mountain fastness that allowed us to take them so completely by surprise. I stroke my new chestnut Arabian mare as she recovers from her indignation at having to change owners at such short notice. Some choice fodder soon persuades her that she's on the right side.

The following night we do the same, but striking at the side instead of the rear, and in the early evening when the men are tired, hungry and eating. Our bowmen put more tents to the torch while our cavalry captures still more supplies and sends pack animals scattering into the night. This time, some arrows come our way, but they bounce off Spartan armour.

For the next two weeks, we continue to snap at their heels and their flanks. Sapping their strength by taking their supplies. Putting the lands in front of them to the torch so they cannot replenish. Stealing their animals from under their noses. Finally, our scouts report that for this night, the Persians have mounted a guard around their sides and rear. So we do nothing and get a good night's sleep ourselves. Knowing that the Persian soldiers will be stressed, sleepless and worn out by morning.

As dark night fades into dawn, stoking the remains of the campfire, Leon says, 'Erebos and his men are going to shadow the Persians on foot and report back. What we do next will depend very much on the territory.' The next day, our forces move in a general westward direction while the Krypteia follow the vast Persian army as invisibly as ghosts. We've captured a huge amount of provisions and fodder, so troops and animals are being well fed. As Leon and I ride together, I'm pondering his remark about territory. And I'm thinking of Xenophon's account of the Ten Thousand when they were blocked trying to cross a river, how he skilfully misled the enemy into thinking and doing the wrong thing.

I say at last, 'You mentioned territory. I think there's a river once we're over the mountains. When I came this way with Philemon and his entourage, it was too deep to ford. And someone had burned the boats.'

'So the Athenian cavalry made rafts?'

'In no time at all. But I can't see the Persians sawing down trees, can you?'

'So they'll look for another crossing point?'

'Yes, like the master and his Ten Thousand. And when they did find a ford, they also found a detachment of the enemy force waiting there for them. That is when he once again employed the art of deception.'

'Fooling the enemy into thinking that most of his men

were going to try and cross at the original point, when in fact they crossed at the ford once the way was clear. And do we think that our friends in baggy trousers are clever enough to work that one out?'

'Let's see, shall we?'

At this point a Krypteian arrives on a lathered horse to report that the Persians are staking out a camp for the night not far from a deep river ten miles from here. The pace quickens as we pass the word back about the plan and hurry to descend from the mountains and onto the river plain. By the time dawn breaks, we've all crossed the river down at the ford, well beyond the enemy's line of sight, while the Persians are camped on the other side. Our bowmen and chariots are lined up along the shore, ready to return fire. While the cavalry wait in the trees to catch any reckless Persians who might try to force a way through.

Leon says, 'You may grumble about their numbers, Wolf Eyes, but three hundred thousand can only cross ten or twenty at a time – *if* they find this ford and *if* we let them cross!'

As a delaying tactic, this buys us several days. And I realise how cumbersome a huge army is. It takes half a day before the Persian leaders realise that the river can't be forded at that point. By the time they've found the ford, it's dark so the scouts return to camp. There then passes another day before a contingent of Persian cavalry arrives at the ford. Only to find our bowmen ready to fire on them. If they had run a concerted charge, there's a chance that one or two might have made it across. But they're in disarray, their horses don't want to enter the water and these troops certainly weren't expecting Sparta on the opposite shore. Once more, they disappear from sight. Presumably back to camp.

In the meantime, the Krypteia have been keeping a close eye on the Persian camp. Erebos reports as we take a hurried meal in the dark. 'A cohort of Persian troops are on the move. Looks like they could be heading for the coast.'

Leon says, 'You and your men need to follow them, Erebos. In case they've guessed where we landed and aim to cut off our retreat. Our ships and men could be in grave danger.'

Erebos says, 'We'll not let that happen.'

'Take whatever supplies you may need. I know the Krypteia like to travel light, but it could help you to travel faster.'

As Erebos disappears, I feel relief that for once, the Persians have done something we're not expecting. This had all been feeling too easy.

*

The river-crossing ambush comes to a head on the fourth day, when the Persian cavalry mount a charge across the ford, with their archers firing a hail of arrows. But the barbs make little impact on our bowmen's bronze armour and cockaded helmets while they mow the Persians down in the water. I wonder at how poorly protected our enemy is, with wicker shields and just thick fabric and leather cuirasses between our iron and their hearts.

As the day goes on, more and more Spartan arrows cause the river to run red. And still these scantily armed Persians come forward to die. What kind of enemy throws its troops so defencelessly into battle and doesn't seem to care how many fall? Finally, night draws the attacks to a close and our troops take some food. I say to Leon, 'If I were the Persians, I'd be looking for another crossing place right now. If they do that, and find one, they'll outflank us.'

'So it's time to move on.'

'Yes. And I've an idea as to where. On the way to the Persian King's court with Philemon, we went through a narrow pass with high cliffs on one side, and a deep, fast river on the other. Then, more cliffs.'

'Another Thermopylae?'

'Narrower. The Athenian cavalry couldn't ride more than four abreast.'

'How long was the road through the gorge?'

'Around five miles.'

'How far from here, would you say?'

'Maybe a day's ride. Or a night's.'

He gets up. 'Night ride it is.'

The men are eager to get going to another point of attack. The seasoned soldiers in this crack force were all thinking the same as us: time to get out before we're penned in like pigs for the slaughter. In no time, we're on the move. The night is fine, with Selene lighting our way through the trees. We have two cavalrymen riding ahead as scouts and two guarding the rear. We're six hours into the ride when a rearguard scout gallops forward to report. A force of maybe two hundred Persians has passed behind us on a direct path to the encampment we had by the river.

When we reach the gorge, dawn is just tinting the dark rocks of the cliffs. Immediately, our troops start to set up, hauling all the gear needed by the bowmen to the top of the cliffs. Meanwhile, Leon sends out scouts to keep a lookout to our rear. Then he and I climb the cliff – a task where Pyro's ingenious leg brace allows me to scramble upwards at some speed. The aim is to identify weak areas on the clifftop where the enemy could approach from behind. What we find is ground that slopes down into foothills, where our cavalry can provide a rearguard action to protect the bowmen.

I say to Leon, 'This ambush could be far more productive in lessening their numbers than the river crossing.'

'And with a good rearguard we could keep it going for as long as it takes.'

We send out scouts to discover if there is any other road than the one through this pass that the Persians can follow. They report back that there is, but many miles to the north. So the Persians are going to have to come this way. We place our bowmen in a concentrated row over the very last few hundred yards of the five-mile route through the gorge, so that by the time they can see the end of the gorge, the Persians will be thinking that they're going to get away with it. Our bowmen are well supplied with arrows because of the quantity of provisions we've been able to bring in the chariots. And they know that what is required here is not volleys of arrows but deadly precision shooting; their targets will be unable to move fast through this narrow defile.

Scouts report that the advancing Persian army has been sighted ten miles away. Plenty of time for our troops to take some food before the action begins. What they won't have had much of is sleep. But as Leon and I walk through their ranks, what we see are men with the glow of battle in their eyes, cheerful and eager to get to grips with this enemy that would make Sparta eat dust. One young archer in particular catches my eye as he cleans his bow with a piece of leather. 'Alessandro, yes?'

He stands to attention. 'Yes, sir.'

'We watched you being crowned victor in the archery competition. Never seen shooting like it.'

'Thank you, sir.'

Leon comments, 'May Apollo and Artemis guide your hands again, soldier.'

'I'll do my best, sir.'

'And we'll do ours – the cavalry has your back down there.'

Shortly after, scouts report that the Persian army is at the entrance to the gorge. Leon and I decide that the best place for us is protecting our bowmen, so we get down to the foothills where the cavalry are patrolling. This is not going to be another Thermopylae, where the treachery of a local man gave away the secret path to the top of the cliff and hordes of Persians outflanked the legendary King Leonidas and his courageous few.

Time drags on and we can see and hear nothing. Then a scout reports that the army has halted at the entrance to the gorge and a contingent of Persian cavalry is approaching the foothills. Leon exclaims, 'Are they, by Zeus!'

In seconds we're in formation. As soon as the Persians come into sight, we go into a flat-out charge, spears pointed. Leon is the first to hurl his spear, with an accuracy that brings the foremost Persian rider to earth with a crash. My spear catches the man behind him in the thigh and he joins his leader in the dust. Now our men are throwing with the precision that we saw them training for in that downhill charge under Xenophon. Leon draws his sword and I draw mine and we prepare for bloody close-quarters combat on horseback. But the remaining Persian riders are wheeling and turning.

Horrified, perhaps, by the ferocity of our attack. Astounded, maybe, that the ambush they feared in the gorge was waiting for them all along here. Now, the only thing the Persian army can do to save themselves from ambush number two is to turn back and take the long way round. But they don't know that.

We all retrieve our spears, the cavalry resumes its patrolling as if nothing has happened, and Leon and I ride back up the slopes to take a look at what is happening down in the gorge. Pulling ourselves on our stomachs to the cliff edge to avoid being seen, we watch an endless column of, first, cavalry riding four abreast, then infantry marching six abreast, three hundred feet below, the deep, swirling river beyond them. Not a man among them that isn't darting nervous glances upwards. Towards the middle of the column, surrounded by a bodyguard, rides a gold-helmeted personage. Leon whispers, 'I wonder if our star bowman will hit that target?'

'They'll wrap him in shields at the first sign of trouble. He's the only one who's not expendable.'

We edge back from the cliff and ride to join our bowmen. Leon informs their leader about the skirmish in the foothills. And then everyone is silent, as we listen to the faint sound of the approaching horses and marching feet far below.

EIGHT

SINGEING THE KING OF PERSIA'S BEARD

At a word from their leader, and in a sequence as synchronised as a well-ordered dance, the bowmen load their weapons, step to the edge of the cliff, take aim and loose their arrows. Then they step back out of sight again to recharge their bows. Looking down, we can see the shock and chaos. The end of the gorge was in sight; the Persians must have thought they were in the clear. Then this murdering rain falls, every bowman shooting with a lethal accuracy. Men are dying, horses are screaming, their cavalry breaks into a gallop and the infantry are running to try and save themselves. In their desperation, some throw themselves into the river but are instantly swept away. The brave Persian archers are letting fly, but it's hopeless, trying to defend yourself against an enemy who is three hundred feet above you, without getting an arrow in the eye.

For most of the day, the blood-letting goes on. There are further skirmishes with our cavalry when groups of infantry at the rear double back in a vain attempt to stop our bowmen's deathly storm. Some try to climb the cliffs but are picked off like swatted flies. When the last Persians have hurried out of this death zone, many with fearful backwards glances to see what else might be pursuing them, our cavalry ride along the pass to get a rough idea of the numbers of the fallen, and to quickly finish off any who are in their last agonies. They return as our troops congregate on the clifftop for a well-earned meal, leaving a contingent to guard the animals and chariots below in the foothills.

Over our campfire, Leon says, 'The numbers of the fallen, our cavalry say, are in the tens of thousands. They could not ride the whole pass because of the blockades of heaped bodies so had to make an educated guess.'

I shrug. 'The perfect ambush?'

Leon looks at me closely. 'There are some who might say that now is the time to return to our ships. To set sail back to Sparta and help prepare for the invasion.'

I'm silent, poking the flames with a stick until the sparks fly. Leon sighs. 'Out with it, Wolf Eyes!'

'Remember Xenophon and the Ten Thousand? When they almost got to Babylon?'

'And would have de-throned the King of Kings if the idiot pretender Cyrus hadn't got himself killed? Where is this leading, Wolf Eyes?'

'First of all, please believe me when I say that I am completely confident that the allies will defeat the Persians when we join battle. We've done it before and we'll do it again. This time, not outnumbered nearly as badly as we were before.'

Leon is still looking at me warily but with a trace of a smile. 'That's the longest speech you've ever made to me. Go on.'

'I want to give the high and mighty Babylon a quick kick in the groin before we go home, and I think I know how.'

Leon laughs. 'Every man here would love to do that! That's how Xenophon picked them. And he will rejoice to hear of it. Let's sleep on it and make an early start.'

The grazing has been good on the hillsides and the animals are well fed and well rested as we make our preparations for a high-speed trajectory to Babylon. Cavalry and bowmen have been well-briefed and are fired up at the idea of teaching the King of Kings a lesson about leaving Persia to make war on Greece. Now, his own home is to come under attack.

As we set off at speed, more than ever I feel pleased at the design of our chariots. We have a highly mobile strike force, capable of carrying abundant provisions and spare weaponry in the chariots, which then double as versatile war machines. To give Balios a break, I'm riding the chestnut Arabian mare plundered from our first attack on the Persian army. I decide to call her Circe, after the sorceress who enchanted Odysseus on his long journey home from Troy. Not only has she an odyssey of a journey to go on, but she'll completely bewitch Arion when she arrives at Danae's estate.

After several days' hard riding, we slow the pace at the approach to the sixty-foot-high walls of Babylon. We have no idea how heavily armed the city might be. What we are planning is an outrageous lightning attack that will set on fire the buildings within those walls. Then, a disappearance as fast as the onslaught. But now, we have to employ Xenophon's arts of deception. So the cavalry spreads out across the plain, because scattered riders do not look like a large force. Each chariot tucks behind a cavalry rider, where it is well-concealed from eyes scanning the plain. We wait until nightfall. Then, we strike.

Every chariot carries a bowman with a flaming arrow, and plenty more with which to recharge his weapon. Many more archers are mounted and use the chariots to re-fire their own bows. Our cavalry are waiting in case the Gate of Ishtar opens to release Babylon's mounted wrath on us. But we know and they know that if that gate opens, and our forces are more powerful than theirs, then they have let the enemy in to wreak havoc. We watch the gate closely, but there is never any sign of it opening. I wonder what the chain of command is when the King of Kings is away. I wonder if they have a chain of command at all in his absence. Or do they have so little imagination and so much arrogance that it never occurs to them what might happen while their king is away, trying to plunder nations who never harmed him until he asked for it.

Once the attack has begun, it is relentless. Flaming arrows fly like meteorites over those high walls in their hundreds and then their thousands. Chariots and riders galloping up to the gate, releasing their fire and then plunging away in the shock and awe tactics they have learned so well. Again and again they come, until the sky above the city takes on an orange glow. I know that the Gate of Ishtar is made of glazed bricks that no fire arrows can ignite. I don't know what the temples and other buildings inside are made of. But it looks like quite a lot is catching fire. On the other side of the walls we can hear shouting. I keep a close eye on the huge gate; if it does start to open, we will switch to our Plan B and form into battalions for an all-out attack. But no one dares to unbar the mighty gate that once trapped me and Philemon inside with the Grand Vizir and his hooded eyes.

Leon gallops up to me on Xanthos, bow in hand. He's enjoying himself, doesn't often get a chance to shoot flaming arrows, and, of course, he's really good at it. 'Are you happy, Wolf Eyes?'

'D'you think they're warm enough in Babylon now?'

'I think we can leave them to it. I'd race you, but I don't think Xanthos would stand a chance with this Arabian mare of yours.'

We recall our troops and start on the long, fast return journey, travelling with only brief halts for food, water and rest for men and animals. When we get to the river where we held off the Persians, Leon briefs the cavalry commander. 'You must now take sufficient chariots with supplies and pursue the invading army while we return by sea. What you must do is cruel but necessary. You must lay waste to the lands that the Persians travel. We must deprive them of provisioning to weaken them further.'

I add, 'In lands that are friendly to Athens and Sparta, they must burn their crops in order not to feed the enemy. They will lose their crops to the Persians anyway if they don't deprive them.' I catch Leon's eye quickly and he nods. 'We will recompense them for their hardship. That is the promise of Athens and Sparta!' Keen for action, the cavalry thunders off; they should overtake the Persians' vast lumbering army in a few days. In darkness, we rally the bowmen and remaining charioteers and set off back to our ships at Troy.

As we travel, I wonder what could be happening on those beaches. With the protection of the Krypteia, our men will be safe from the size of cohort that set off from the Persian army. But the big question in our minds now is, where is the King of King's fleet? In the last invasion, the fleet shadowed the army's overland route, staying relatively close to the shore. Although this didn't stop them getting trashed in some severe storms. So, have there been any sightings of what must be one of the largest fleets the Aegean has ever seen?

When we reach the shores of Troy in dawn's dim light we find an empty beach. Leon says, 'They will have been warned by the Krypteia and put out to sea.' Leaving the men to rest, he and I climb the cliff to where we can look out westwards over the ocean. He points to a distant sail. 'There they are! Thank Poseidon for that!' We wave our scarlet cloaks in the breeze and the sun flashes on a sword raised on the ship. Half an hour later, all our triremes are safely beached and our small army is loading. I say to Damon, 'Did you have any unwelcome visitors?'

'Erebos got us well out of the way before the Persian cohort arrived.'

I don't ask if he knows where the Krypteia went; no one in this world or the next knows the answer to that. 'Have you seen any sign of the Persian fleet?'

He shakes his head. 'No, and I don't expect to, Commander.'

'You're thinking, they won't repeat the pattern of the last invasion?'

'That is what everyone will be expecting them to do.'

I look at him closely. 'If you were commanding that fleet, what would be your plan, Damon?'

'I would head through the Cyclades, like the first invasion did. But I would only use the islands for provisioning. I wouldn't sack them; plenty of time for that later. I would pay for their supplies and promise alliances and future trade.'

'I'm with you. Because Athens is the prize. So you would break with this pattern at, say, Naxos, and head southwards around Laconia?'

'Yes, Commander. Then I'd turn northwards along the western coast of Greece and into the Gulf of Corinth. Lay waste to Athens' naval shipyards and provide the perfect blockade for any Greeks wishing to evacuate the city from the Persian troops who are by then filling the plains.'

Leon has been listening intently. 'Yours is a very good theory, Damon. And I'm sure that most ships in the Persian fleet will be doing exactly as you say. Could be several thousand or more. But suppose that the Persians also wish to mislead us into thinking that their fleet is following exactly the same route that it did in the last invasion?'

'Using deceit to distract from the real invasion? Not difficult; you may see only a hundred ships on the horizon, but there could be many hundreds more beyond. Or not.'

I look at Leon. 'So first our ships need to shadow the army's land route?'

'The Krypteia should have gathered some intelligence when we meet them next.'

'But we desperately need information from the south if the main fleet could be heading that way!'

'The Athenian patrols could already have sighted the Persians – we'll only find out when we get back.'

Poseidon is in a grumpy mood as we struggle to get off the lee shore. In a rising wind, hordes of us have to jump into the water and push the ships into the sea to help the oarsmen get enough depth to make some way. Add to that clusters of puffy dark clouds massing on the horizon, and it looks like the next twenty-four hours are going to be interesting.

The storm hits with the force of a clenched fist from Poseidon, blasting our ships until they're forced to take down their sails. Our valiant rowers battle into the waves, lightning dancing off the masts, but this is a fight we're not going to win. Damon signals to the fleet to turn towards the nearest shore to save ourselves. Ships rolling perilously, we head towards what the lightning strikes show up as a small, sheltered cove. Damon shouts a warning as rocks appear amid the foam. Most of the ships land safely and are dragged up the beach away from the waves. But one boat starts travelling helplessly sideways in a huge wave and hits a rocky outcrop, stoving in its hull.

Instantly a rescue mission is underway, with men swimming out to get animals and soldiers to shore. In freezing rain and lashing gales, we shelter behind the boats until a gradually calming grey dawn shows. As soon as that happens, Leon and I are gone – scouting along the clifftop to see if we have neighbours. The bay next to our small cove is maybe a mile wide, sheltered by headlands and with broad, level beaches. In the sea mist that accompanies the dawn, we can see on those beaches around one hundred Persian triremes. Joining them, in twos and threes from the open ocean, are more ships from Persia's far-flung dominions. And doubtless, more to come. But how many more? Is this the Persians' decoy fleet? Or is it the main fleet gathering, ready to follow the previous coastal course and doing the opposite of what we are calculating?

The crews are obviously expecting only allies and looking no further than the bay. So they don't see the Krypteia rise up like ghosts from the wind-blown bushes on the top of the cliff. Erebos engages in conversation with Leon and me. 'No, we haven't sent any birds yet; it wasn't at all clear what was happening.'

'We're far from clear as well,' says Leon, 'but we need to warn the allies that there could be a Persian naval deceit underway.'

I say, 'If Damon is right, surely our first message needs to urge tight patrols through the Cyclades to look for the Persians' main fleet heading for Corinth? Several thousand ships can't hide. And if they *are* there they mustn't know we've found them!'

Erebos agrees. 'We can remain here to keep the Persians under observation. If we can have one of your ships, we can shadow them when they leave. And send word of the fleet size and course as soon as they become apparent.'

The birds fly with our first message within minutes. Erebos and his men drag one of the triremes up onto the shore so that it cannot be seen from the clifftop. Then they disappear into the dawn to watch the Persians in the next bay. Shortly afterwards, our little navy is slipping out of the cove, grateful for the cold, damp fog that cloaks us. Our oarsmen dip almost silently until we're well out of hearing. As an offshore breeze catches us, we raise the sails and head for Greece. Behind us lies what we believe is the Persians' decoy fleet, gathering its numbers in a bay just ten miles north of Troy. And far south, heading for the Cyclades, could be the massive force with which the King of Kings aims to crush the warships of Greece.

*

Poseidon blows strong but kindly winds for the rest of our five-day voyage back to Sparta. As we beach the ships and unload the horses and chariots, Xenophon is waiting on his white charger. On the way back to Danae's estate, he has important news. 'Much has moved forward in your absence. Athens and Sparta have formed an alliance and are in conversation with many others who wish to join them in standing as one against the Persian foe. I received your message and Philemon immediately shared it with the Athens assembly. The Athenian and Spartan fleets now stand ready for deployment either as one or more forces. Allied ships are patrolling the northern coastline, and scouts are monitoring the progress of the Persian army.'

'So no sightings of the Persians' main fleet as yet, Master?'

'Not as yet.'

Back at the estate, I hand Circe's lead rope to Danae with a bow. She looks at the Arabian appraisingly. Knowing an expert when she sees one, the golden chestnut stands at her full elegance, legs four square, neck and tail gracefully arched. Danae murmurs, 'Oh my, you are a clever girl.' She leads the mare around the manege to check out her general health and see how she moves before taking her to the stables for food and water. Circe puts on a show for Danae that she never bothered to with me, with the airy dancing walk that I so love in Arion. Then Zena comes out and takes in the new arrival. 'Is this your present from Persia, Lycon?'

'With the compliments of the King of Kings. She's come a long way; I call her Circe.'

She laughs with delight. 'The lady who bewitched Odysseus!'

'Just wait till Arion sees her!'

Sitting at Danae's dining table with the master, our debrief takes a while. Unsurprisingly, Xenophon is particularly interested in numbers, and we do our best. Having been vague about the torching of the tents on the plain and the river blockade, when we get to the gorge ambush, all we can do is reiterate what the cavalry said. When I get to the firing of Babylon, I wonder if the master might reproach me for wasting manpower in a silly gesture. But he approves: 'The psychological importance of that fire raid is immense. A warning given to our aggressors. No Greek lives lost. Resources well spent.' He pauses, then adds, 'In fact, your tally of Greek lives lost currently reads at zero, does it not?'

Leon says, 'We had some injuries when a trireme foundered, but all men and animals were saved, sir.'

This brings us to the finding of what could be the Persian decoy fleet and our conversation with Damon about the possible route and target of the main fleet. The master comments, 'This commander is a man with a keen understanding of naval strategy.'

Leon says, 'So you think he's right, Master?'

'Ever since your message arrived, we have been patrolling the Cyclades. Athens has a fleet of three hundred ships in the Gulf of Corinth.'

I reply, 'But by the time a scout ship gets back with the news that the Persian fleet has been sighted, they could have sent in an overwhelming force to tear the Athenian fleet to pieces.'

Xenophon's grey eyes look straight at mine. 'What do you want to do, Lycon?'

'I think we have to trust that Damon is right and get underway with the Spartan fleet tomorrow.'

Leon says quietly, 'You have a plan, don't you, Wolf Eyes?'

'It goes like this. We sail in line just within sighting distance of each other, so not obviously a naval force. The first ship to sight the Persian fleet flies a red cloak from the mast and the message gets passed down the line. As soon as the cloak is flown the fleet starts to take battle formation. But we don't engage yet; we stay out of sight of the Persians, with just one scout ship keeping an eye on them.'

Xenophon murmurs, 'Because battle in close conditions works to our advantage.'

'As Themistocles said before Salamis, Master.'

'You want them to go right into the gulf, don't you, Wolf Eyes?'

'Yes, Leon. To find the Athenian fleet waiting for them, and Sparta behind them.'

'While there should be plenty of allied warships to deal with the decoy fleet when it arrives.'

I say, 'We should have further information from the Krypteia before long. So the allies could maybe act before the decoy fleet arrives.'

Xenophon looks at me with a slight smile. 'You are acquiring a reputation as the master of the pre-emptive strike, Lycon.'

I blush with embarrassment but Leon agrees, 'And that way we get to choose the battle arena.'

*

The very next day, as we're making hurried preparations to get the Spartan fleet underway, Zena is seen on Arion as he picks his way down the cliff path; she's carrying another exhausted pigeon. Leon's eyes light up as he reads. 'It's as we thought! Erebos says it must be a decoy fleet as only three hundred ships in total have set sail, including supply. He gives their course.'

Xenophon takes the message from him. 'This is timely news. I will pass it on to the allies while you go in search of the main fleet.'

After the intensive shipbuilding programme, the Spartan triremes massing in the bay number three hundred. All of them one hundred and twenty feet long, each with a ten-foot, bronze-clad ram and all driven by powerful young men who have been training for months for this chance to bend to their oars in pursuit of Persian prey. So we now have a fleet equal in size to our Athenian brothers'. The fact that Athens' and Sparta's fleets are each only the size of the Persian decoy fleet is not something that we lose sleep over.

Damon, our admiral, is carrying out last-minute briefings with the trireme commanders. Leon and I are rowing on his warship named *Eagle*, painted with fierce golden eyes on the prow; the lethal ram juts out like a giant beak, ready to tear its prey to pieces. We pull out of the bay ahead of the fleet and begin the journey southwards under a cloudless sky, a steady breeze filling the sails. We have around 250 miles of the Aegean to cross before we are south of the Cyclades. Anywhere along that route, one of our ships could spot the Persian fleet.

As we head out to sea, the ships start to distance themselves so that we're just within sight of each other. They're fanning out too, across a three-mile stretch. Like Xenophon says, if you space yourselves out, you don't look like a large force; you may barely look like a force at all. He was writing about cavalry, but the same applies to ships.

Some of the men we're rowing with took me across the sea to Piraeus on my spying mission and there's a lot of friendly banter now that I'm shoulder to shoulder with them. Leon and I just take it for granted that Damon is the man in charge here. This might be my plan, but the original idea was his. And only he has the seamanship, the knowledge and a deep understanding of the invading Persian navy. Free of a commanding role, I love to feel the ship powering through the waves again, with those silvery flying fish our escorts through the blue Aegean. I look at Leon, but he seems preoccupied, just pulling hard on his oar.

The crew are also seasoned fishermen, taking it in turns to catch fish and roast the flesh. I eat more fish on the *Eagle* than I ever have in my life. My normal diet is bread and cheese, with figs and olives if I'm lucky. But the meat that the crew catch is delicious and good for body building. After another fish meal, Leon teases me that my muscles are toning up so fast with the rowing that I'll start to get fat. I retort, 'What about you, then? Zena swears that you'll be putting on weight with many more meals at Danae's house!'

I seem to have struck a nerve because Leon goes quiet at his oar. Then he says between strokes, with none of his usual confidence, 'Do you think, Wolf Eyes, that Danae and Xenophon… Would it be better if I kept out of the way?'

'Why would you want to do that?'

'You can see why, surely. There is a very special friendship between them. I would not wish to intrude… if…' His voice falters. Stunned at his question, I think back to that reunion between Zena and me, after two years of being apart, when I first met Danae and saw her and Leon together. It was at Danae's estate, in her dining room, after Zena had so spectacularly won her chariot race. I saw Danae looking at Leon. And I wondered if it was about more than their plans for Zena. Thinking about it now, the way she looked at him was about a great deal more than that. And thinking about all the other times when I've seen them together… 'You're in love with her, aren't you?'

He whispers, 'I shouldn't dare to hope. She is worlds above me.'

'I'll take that as a yes. Now take this from me. There is only one being that Lady Danae looks at like she wouldn't care if this world was empty of everyone else. That being is not Xenophon, it's not me and it's not any of her horses. Got that?'

Leon is silent at his oar again. But he throws me a glance and his eyes are so bright, it's definitely not sea spray.

I continue, 'It's a professional relationship between Lady Danae and Xenophon. He's been helping her train Zena to win races. She's been helping us to win this war by providing horsepower.'

As I speak, there comes a shout from our helm: 'Red flag southwards!' And there it is: the flash of crimson on the horizon. Instantly, we're pulling like madmen to make battle formation. Word is being relayed through the fleet about the numbers of the Persian ships. Scouts have counted well over one thousand triremes – could be up to fifteen hundred. They number the Persians' lesser fighting ships and their supply ships at three thousand. That, against our three hundred Spartan triremes. With another three hundred Athenian warships lying in wait off Corinth. The usual odds against the Persians, nothing new at all.

To make matters worse, or quite possibly better, Poseidon is far from finished with his fun and games. As we mass into battle-fleet formation, the wind is rising and the sky darkening. Damon surveys the gathering gloom. 'This kind of wind can blow for days.' So the sails come down and the rowers prepare for the long haul, non-stop power if we're going to keep our ship straight at waves that are rapidly approaching twelve feet in height. The one-hundred-and-twenty-foot length of our ship can ride out these waves as long as we take them head-on. Leon mutters as we strain at our oars, 'Once this wind catches up with the Persians it could help to lower the odds!'

'And Antilochus told me that most Persians don't know how to swim.'

During that endless bout with Poseidon, he flung gales, thunder and enormous waves at us, lightning dancing off the masts of the ships. We could not count the days, because days were as dark as night. We could not stop rowing, because that would have turned us sideways to the waves and pitched us into the abyss. We could not eat or drink because we dared not take our blistered hands from the oars. We listened to Damon's shouts of encouragement like they were a lifeline above the banshee screams of the gale.

When the winds finally subside, he tells us that the gales blew for five days before we drifted into these calm blue seas. The men are exhausted and supplies of water are desperately low, so the fleet briefly puts into a friendly Cycladean island. When they hear who we're looking for, the islanders heap provisions on us. As we set sail again, they're making a burnt sacrifice on the beach and praying to Zeus.

We don't have to wonder for very long how the Persian fleet weathered Poseidon's displeasure. As soon as we enter the main straits that will take us towards Sparta, the lookouts are shouting warnings about large pieces of debris floating just below the surface. First there's an oar, then many oars. Then a mast with the sail still attached, followed by the upturned hull of a Persian trireme.

Then it's not just pieces of ship: it's bodies, floating face down. And despite my cheap joke, I hate to see any foe defeated in this way, annihilated by a force that no human could resist. Even if these poor wretches had been able to swim, there was nowhere for them to save themselves. It would just have made their deaths more long, drawn out. I wish we could at least give them the dignity of a burial, but there's nothing we can do to prevent the sea from claiming them for its own.

It's impossible to estimate by how much Poseidon has lowered the odds for us. The wreckage goes on for mile after mile. Sickened by the carnage, I pull fiercely on my oar. Pulling beside me, Leon says, 'It could just as well have been us, Wolf Eyes.'

I growl, 'We don't need these endless wars to tear men from their families – why doesn't the King of Persia just throw all his soldiers off a cliff and have done with it!'

'He doesn't care for his men like Xenophon does. He doesn't train or arm or protect them properly, just relies on numbers.'

Then we're both silent as the grim relics continue to float past our ship. The fleet is fully back in formation now. All of us wondering when and where we will catch up with our prey. All of us hoping that the prey remains in complete ignorance of the wolves on its tail.

*

We row onwards for days before turning northwards to hug the shores of Western Greece, and still there are no sails on the horizon. Then we get a strong southerly wind that we can run with for many miles and Damon sends the two fastest ships ahead to try and get a sighting. Two days later they return with news: the Persian fleet is entering the Gulf of Corinth. Damon looks shocked that they are so far ahead. Despite the storm, their numbers are still certain to be overwhelmingly vast for the Athenians. That favourable southerly is still blowing when he orders the oarsmen to give it everything they've got and then more. We must close the gap if we want the Athenian fleet to survive.

Hands bleeding with blisters that haven't had a chance to heal, shoulders and arms creaking with cramps, but fired by the knowledge that the foe is almost in sight, we all throw ourselves into the task. Leon gives me a quick grin. 'Happy, Wolf Eyes?'

'You asked me at Babylon. Ask me again at Corinth!'

Now our warships are slicing through the waves, the warm southerly on our backs. We have anger in our hearts. We are ready to engage with the might of the King of Kings.

NINE

'NOW IS THE STRUGGLE FOR ALL THINGS'

Aeschylus, The Persians, 405

We rowed all day and all that night without a pause. During the day, Poseidon stiffened the winds to a gale, but we rejoiced in the force that was pushing us onwards. At night we had the blessing of Selene's silver light to help us keep clear of rocks and reefs as we hugged the shoreline. A fury drives us on, firing our limbs with power, making us immune to muscle cramps and exhaustion. And we are rewarded. As dawn pours rosy light across the horizon, Damon shouts, 'The Gulf! Now to it, men, and we shall soon be on them!'

A roar goes up and we grasp our oars with redoubled energy. Our ship *Eagle* is the first to round the headland into the Gulf of Corinth – and there are some twenty stragglers from the main Persian fleet ahead. In full battle formation, the first line charges; our ship heads exactly parallel to the enemy trireme and our ram cleaves through the whole length of their oars like they're made of straw. So they can't manoeuvre to get out of the way as the ship following us smashes its beak into the side of their hull with such force that it capsizes them. While the first two ships move on to the next prey, the third delivers the death blow into the stern of the stricken vessel and it's all over for them.

This tactic works supremely well, again and again, as we penetrate deeper into the gulf and start to catch up with the vast numbers of the main enemy fleet. In fact, it works even better amongst the packed Persian ships, as they just don't have the room to manoeuvre. We also have the huge advantage of surprise, as it takes them a while to realise that wolves are savaging the rear of their fleet. So while we pick off our victims, sometimes with just one lethal high-speed thrust of the ram, they are powerless to turn and mount a rearguard action.

This is like fighting the pirates, except that there are so many vulnerable Persian ships out there, all of them facing in the wrong direction, that it seems almost too easy. Certain that the weather or our fortunes could turn any time, we get stuck in. Charging and wrecking, again and again. I can hardly believe how seldom we are challenged. It would seem that the Persian navy is only used to advancing in one direction, with its full might pointing one way. Just like when we torched their tents at night during their advance, they had no idea that an enemy could dare to break the conventions of battle like this.

Rowing next to Leon, I say, 'Like you said, there are no rules of warfare anymore. The enemy always formulated them to suit themselves – no reason for anyone to obey them.'

He replies, 'So keep on breaking the rules, Wolf Eyes. It's working!'

I've lost count of the ships that we've sunk and I'm straining to look ahead to see how close to the Athenian shipyards we might be, when Leon points across the water. Some thirty Persian ships are peeling away from the main fleet. 'Probably trying to outflank us.'

'Poor wretches don't know what they're heading into.'

What the poor wretches are doing is setting themselves up as easy targets, broadside on to our triremes, as they try to get behind us. Damon shouts commands to the ships in the line behind ours to close up and take our place. Then *Eagle*, along with four other warships, launches itself like a fury at the Persian cohort. We head for the centre of the Persian line to break it up, ploughing into five of their ships and almost riding over the tops of them as they sink beneath the waves with vast holes in their hulls.

Then our squadron of five turns and takes aim at the head of their fleet. There is nothing they can do to defend themselves. Our ships are heading towards them with such colossal power and speed that even if they try to turn, we just shear off their oars with our ram then go in for the death blow. We take on the next five ships and then the next, with similar results. The only lesson the Persians might have learned from trying to outflank us was – don't. Because they exposed themselves fatally to experienced sea warriors who were well used to such tactics. And I am beginning to feel a great pity for the Persians.

As our little flotilla prepares to resume battle with the main fleet, Damon is looking at a commotion at the front. At first it's impossible to see what is happening, until he calls, 'The Athenians are attacking, pushing the Persians back onto their own ships!' And my heart stirs as I think of Antilochus and his mighty waterborne army, dealing out death blows for Athens. So we've reached the Persian navy in time to join forces with our Athenian allies.

Damon decides that our band of five warships can now be of most use at the rear, cutting off Persians who try to flee or regroup. So we row in tight formation and lie in wait for any change in tactics on the part of the Persians. But having witnessed the fate of their first expedition, they evidently decide to press on regardless. With the truly vast numbers of the Persian fighting ships, whatever they decide, they are going to regret it. The battle rages all day and continues into the night under the light of a blazing full moon; Selene is with us once again, at the height of her powers. Damon decides to keep our rearward position, where we have a good view of the battle and can come to the aid of Spartan or Athenian as soon as we spot a problem.

I've been trying to work out just why the Persians are losing so many warships when – as usual with this foe – we are losing so few. Like he's reading my mind, Leon says, 'Their hearts are not in it, Wolf Eyes. Here we have Greeks forgetting old grudges to fight for their freedom, under a leadership that will never recklessly take them to battle. On the opposing side, we have men who are poorly trained and equipped, and forced to fight far from home and family for a king who cares nothing for them.' I consider his words; it's the longest speech I've ever heard from Leon. And yet it is truly laconic, with every single phrase resonating and not a word wasted. Like the voice of my little pupil, in her scorn of the squabbling gods, I can still hear him.

The sea is littered with wreckage when we finally see cohorts of Persian ships break away, trying to leave the gulf. But even in retreat, they must be stopped; they can't be allowed to regroup. So Spartan ships join with Athenian in relentlessly pursuing and sinking the deserters. At one point, Damon and Antilochus are commanding ships racing in parallel after a heavily armed cluster of Persian triremes. Rowing manically on Damon's ship, Leon and I exchange looks – it must be just like the old days, when they chased pirates together.

The Persians have put up a brave front during the day. But they don't like fighting at night, whether they're on land or at sea. So the pincer action of Spartans at the rear of their fleet and Athenians at the front, with deserters ruthlessly pursued and sunk, works with chilling effectiveness. But I hate it that the King of Kings can't be bothered to train his sailors to swim. The worst that would have happened to those who managed to swim to shore would have been slavery. As it was, there were countless bodies drifting face down in the sea or washed up on the beach. That is not the way to treat people who you ask to lay down their lives for you.

By dawn, the shores and the waters around them are completely blocked with splintered carcasses of ships and drowned bodies. So a massive clear-up operation gets underway, with Athenian citizens lending their slaves and carriages to cart the wooden and human wreckage away and light giant pyres. The dark smoke coils into the grey skies as the Athenian and Spartan warships are beached and warriors deployed out onto the lines that are forming to defend the city in the final battle.

Waiting for Leon and me as we help to haul our victorious *Eagle* trireme up the beach are two old friends who have not enjoyed each other's company for a long time. Philemon embraces me like a son. 'My dear Lycon!'

'My dear master. It is so very good to see you again!'

My brother-in-arms bows deeply to Philemon and says in his quiet voice, 'Sparta has much to thank you for, sir.'

'Athens is profoundly grateful that she has the might of Sparta with her in this struggle, Leon. I have always wanted it so.'

'And now,' says Xenophon, 'we must arm and to the field. We wouldn't want to keep the King of Kings waiting.'

*

We spend the rest of the day on the plains outside Athens, establishing battle formations and briefing our commanders. Then our troops are told to eat and drink their fill from the abundant provisions that the Athenians have supplied. As evening casts its grey cloak over the campfires, scouts report that the Persian army has positioned itself two miles away.

Our troops are on the vantage point, on the high ground nearer to the city; more are joining every hour from the allies.

The Krypteia are now our most deadly agents once again. Drifting like ghosts through the Persian camp to find out where the King of Kings resides. Counting numbers of cavalry, infantry and bowmen. Looking closely at the lie of the land over which the Persian army must advance. Taking account of any vantage points they might try to gain, and of potential weaknesses that our troops can exploit.

Then, a mile from the enemy camp, Erebos and his men set about making life difficult for the Persian cavalry. Felling trees, digging ditches, even diverting streams: creating all the obstacles they can to slow the enemy's advance. Occasionally through the night comes a flicker of lightning, followed by a rumble of thunder, indicating that the weather too could be among our allies.

We also know that the longer spears and heavier armour of our bronze-clad infantry have prevailed before over the short spears, wicker shields and padded clothing of the Persians. And while the Persian style of fighting usually involves trying to wear their enemy down with a barrage of arrows before closing in with spear and sword, our infantry have been rigorously trained to counter this strategy. The armed race was originally run in the Olympics after the Greeks first came into contact with Persian archery. This athletic event is run over a distance of thirteen hundred feet – enough to take the Greek hoplites through the beaten zone of the enemy arrows and right up to the Persian lines, with the runners wearing helmets, armour and carrying their shields. It develops great strength, speed and stamina: and on the battlefield it can break the famed Persian archers.

After Erebos has reported back to us, he and his men disappear like wraiths into the night. And now, with the campfire dying down, Xenophon's voice drops to a whisper. 'I regret to have to tell you both that there is a risk in addition to the vast army gathered not far from us.'

Leon says, 'Our two kings?'

Xenophon's eyes are looking beyond the dimming firelight. 'The ephors and I have agreed that in the forming of this alliance with Athens, we cannot allow the Athenians to know of our lack of trust in the pair of them. One, in particular.'

Leon asks, 'Erastus?'

'Up to his old tricks again, I'm afraid. He insists that the Spartan army needs strengthening by recruiting a cohort of mercenaries. The ephors and I are in agreement with King Phidias that this is not necessary. However, Erastus has managed to communicate his views to the Athens assembly and they support him.'

'Do the ephors know how he's managed to act so independently?'

'No, Leon. And, with the Krypteia so taken up with matters of war, the usual close surveillance has not been possible.'

I look at Leon, 'So, he must have been in secret meetings with whoever is going to command these mercenaries. Have we any guess as to who that might be?'

Leon says, 'When we exiled Hipparchos, our information is that he went first to Macedon then on to Thrace. Who are vassals of the Persians.'

Now my blood really does run cold. 'You mean, Erastus could have been recruiting a gang of mercenaries who will turn and cut our throats when it suits them?'

Xenophon's voice is calm. 'We can make sure they never get that chance – provided that our generals are forewarned. They can keep the mercenaries in the front line, where they can provide useful fodder for the Persian archers before our hoplites run in to the attack.'

I'm still playing catch-up. 'But what is the real agenda of Erastus? Does he want King Phidias murdered?'

Leon's voice is hard. 'Very likely. Once this war is over, we will need to deal with him. But we cannot afford to let Athens sense any cracks in our ranks; it would understandably shatter their trust in us.'

I'm like a dog with a bone that it can't let go. 'What about Phidias? Does he know what danger he's in? Can we pull him out of it?'

Leon says, 'He will never pull out; he is too proud. I will warn him of the danger he is in and get his bodyguard reinforced.'

But I can only think of the would-be king, Cyrus, who hurtled to his own destruction in his war against the Persians, despite all advice and all attempts to protect him.

*

The briefing goes ahead just after midnight and is passed from cohort to cohort. The Spartans will form the right flank of all battle formations, where their legendary strength and discipline will provide a wall of iron. Precise formations will depend upon territory, but it is agreed that the Spartan cavalry will lead charges on rough and hilly terrain, where their charioteers and bowmen have outstanding skills as well as the Achilles chariot war machine. On level ground, both the Athenian and the Spartan armies will continue to provide the strength of the phalanx, that juggernaut of raw manpower, each man shielding the one next to him, his spear powered on by the rows of men pushing ferociously behind him.

Xenophon has also been in deep discussion with Spartan and Athenian commanders about the importance of tailoring the phalanx to varying depths according to the territory and the way the enemy has positioned themselves. Always with a view to deceiving them as to our own strength and plans.

And so, one bright dawn on the plains outside Athens, a massed army of Spartans bred only for war joins with thousands of armed Athenians and their allies, and together we prepare to meet the enemy who would make us eat dust. To the south, we have the river – deep, fast and impassable. To the north, the mountains and the foothills beneath. And we have plans for our cavalry and our chariots and bowmen in those foothills, while the Persian cavalry struggles with all the obstacles that the Krypteia have placed in their way.

Erebos arrives with a final report on numbers. 'Well down on the original three hundred thousand, sir. The wolves we set on them in Persia, and the starvation rations they have been reduced to from the torching of the land, have cut them to two hundred thousand, we reckon.'

With our numbers nowhere near six figures, we see the Persian army fill the plain. From mountain foothills to the north as far as the river to the south, the sun twinkles on their helmets and sabres. And yet we have learned from history that sheer numbers can quickly become mere numbers. And thanks to the exertions of our early strike force backed by the Krypteia, they have lost one third of what they were.

Xenophon says to me, 'Leon will stay to guard the king and command the phalanx. You will lead the chariots and cavalry far into the foothills and outflank the Persian infantry. Get behind them and beside them, and drive them together and towards us, so that we can smash them with a deep phalanx formation.'

I set off at a canter with the Spartan cavalry and chariots bristling with bowmen in tight formation. Taking a wide arc to avoid making it too obvious what we're doing, we're soon pounding through the foothills, the big-wheeled chariots riding effortlessly over the rough ground. Two mounted Krypteian scouts are ahead of us and at one point they advise us to halt while they check out a possible ambush point where a vertical cliff dominates a narrow pass.

They tell me that at the top of this cliff are many loose boulders, which could form the perfect attack on vulnerable troops. I ride with them to take a look at the pass. It looks dangerous; I send more men to secure the upper heights in case of ambush.

While we wait, the weather fulfils the promises of last night, changing in a few minutes from bright sunlight to increasing darkness, as clouds blot out the sun and a gale starts to blow. There's a violent drop in temperature, followed by a bombardment of hail; the huge hailstones cause the horses to start and toss their heads.

The Krypteians return with the all-clear; they found no one on the clifftops. I wave the men on: 'The Persians won't like the weather – they can't hide in their tents!' There's laughter from the men who torched the tents during the Persian foray and we continue our advance. Rain is now falling in torrents, running in muddy rivulets down the sides of the cliff. Loosened by the sudden intense downpour, some small rocks rumble down the cliff face. It's a relief when we're clear of the pass.

Another canter in tight formation through two miles of foothills and the scouts return to report that we'd be able to see the rear of the Persian army if it wasn't for the thunderous clouds and blinding rain. But that means the Persian army can't see us. Quickly, our cohorts take the formation that they've practised so many times before: bowmen in the centre ranks, cavalry on each of their flanks. Then we're trotting forwards until we can see helmets through the veil of water. I shout the watchword, 'Zeus Saviour, Heracles Leader!'; it's roared back through the ranks as we charge.

The Persians are taken completely by surprise when a storm of Spartan arrows starts to rain death and destruction at their rear. As weaker troops are usually placed at the back, a great many of them make a run for it. We let them go, pressing forward relentlessly, downing their advancing infantry with arrow, spear and sword. As the Persian cavalry is in their usual place at the front of their ranks, they don't even know what's happening.

The battering torrents continue and the ground is becoming a sea of churned mud. Now the middle ranks are becoming aware of the murderous force that is taking them from behind. But you can't start a rearguard action when you're advancing into battle. They have no option but to press onwards, crushed relentlessly together by our cavalry and bowmen on either side: and with the mighty Greek phalanx just waiting until their line starts to break.

Amid the slashing, stabbing and deaths by whistling arrow, I try to make out how we're progressing but I can't see beyond the chaos. Balios is using all his power and agility to negotiate the mud, when I catch a glimpse of an elaborate helmet positioned right in the centre of the heavily armed troops ahead. And I'm pretty sure I know who that is.

Then the rain eases slightly and I see the serried shields and spears of the huge Greek phalanx waiting for their prey. The devastation wreaked by our cavalry and bowmen has narrowed the Persian line so much that it is no longer outflanking the Greek infantry. And the phalanx is now on the move. The going is easier for them as it is untrodden ground. Whereas here, Persians are going down in the greasy mud whether or not they've been felled by iron. I shout to the men, 'To the phalanx, to shield its flanks!' And I'm certain that our old design of chariot could never have made it through that mud bath. But the iron tyres grip and the noble Thessalians handle the ground like they would desert sand.

As we arrive alongside the first rows of the phalanx, Xenophon on his white charger signals urgently to me. Calling to the men to continue supporting the phalanx, I ride over to him. His face is grave and I know that something dreadful has happened. 'King Phidias is dead, murdered by the mercenaries who turned on him and his bodyguard. I am concerned for Leon. He dealt a death sentence to the ring-leader then went after the rest when they fled. Xanthos returned without him an hour ago.'

'Which way?'

'Into the mountains.'

'Alone?'

'Those were his orders – he did not want to take more men away from the fight.'

'Then I must find him!'

'Yes, you must. And Lycon?'

'Yes, sir?'

'The Persian king is in the centre ranks, is he not?'

'I believe I saw him, sir.'

'Then you can tell Leon that the Persian king will die today.'

'And our traitor King Erastus tonight, sir!'

With flying hooves, Balios carries me towards the foothills of the mountains where we travelled eight hours since. Behind us, the battle rages on as the flower of the Persians meets the crushing force of the phalanx. The rain is finally easing and the wind force falling, but it is bitter cold.

I know without thinking too hard what has probably happened. Cowards who are running away will only turn on their pursuer if they know they can do so in safety. I remember the mountain pass where the Krypteia scouted ahead in case of ambush, the perfect place for one. All those loose boulders at the top of the cliff. A fury burns in my chest as I feel the hilt of my sword.

The sun is sinking in blood-red fire as I pause at the entrance to the pass. Balios stands perfectly still as I take in the sides of the cliff to my right, the steep walls where those small rocks tumbled as my men made good their passage through. My gaze travels down the walls until it stops at the devastation below. An avalanche of large boulders has been loosed and is lying in the gully, which is still running with water after the storms.

Balios' ears are pricked; he can hear something which I can't. As I draw my sword, he whirls round and I see them, knives at the ready. I can hear Leon's words in my head and his final lesson of the day… *when all you have left for a fight on horseback is your sword.* It's as though my arm barely belongs to me, so swiftly does the blade sever the heads of the two men who were creeping up behind to kill me, who may have killed Leon. It reminds me of Zena banging the heads together of the men who stole our sheep, so quickly they never knew what happened. Only these two are not going to get up again.

Feeling supernaturally calm, I walk Balios on into the pass, towards the wreckage of boulders. If there were any further mercenaries watching from the top of the cliff, the fate of their comrades will have driven them away. We've reached the boulders and Balios can go no further. Sliding off him, I start to clamber over the slippery rocks. It's almost dark now. I whisper, 'Leon? Come on, this is no time for hide and seek!'

From out of the shadows to my left comes his quiet voice. 'I would have thought it ideal.'

He's lying with his left leg trapped below the knee beneath a huge boulder. The rest of him looks unscathed, but I hate to think what has happened to his leg. I don't think I have a chance in Hades of shifting the rock, but I give it my best shot. It doesn't move.

He says lightly, 'I was jealous of your leg. You always got more attention from the ladies, so now I've gone one better.'

I clamber down and sit beside him, taking his hand. It's ice-cold. 'This isn't good. I need to warm you up.' I raise him enough to put his head on my chest, my cloak wrapped round him, hugging him to my body. 'Can you feel your leg?'

'At first, far too much. Now, not at all.'

'Help will come. You just need to stay alive.'

He laughs. 'Easy.'

'And stay awake.'

'I wasn't thinking of taking a nap.'

'Good. Because if I see you drifting off, I'll have to wake you up.'

'How will you do that?'

'I might have to sing to you. It just might have to come to that.'

'You've never sung to me before.'

'I've never had to keep you awake before.'

'If I go to sleep, do you think I might die?'

'I just think it's better to concentrate on staying alive. You can't do that when you're asleep.'

'Like the time when you went for your walk by the River Styx?'

'And you woke me up, didn't you?'

'It was purely opportunistic. We couldn't have you carrying your news to the grave, could we?'

'How *did* you get into my head?'

'It's something you learn when you've been in the Krypteia for a while. Helps when you're interrogating people. Doesn't always work.'

'Glad it worked for me.' We're silent for a while. Then I feel Leon's breathing becoming shallower with the onset of sleep. So I do what I've threatened and start to sing Lydia's flying horse song as best I can. As the song comes to an end, his head stirs on my chest. I take his hand; it feels warmer than before.

He murmurs, 'I didn't know that singing was among your many talents, Wolf Eyes.'

'There has to be something that you don't know about me.'

'Does there? Can you tell me who wrote the song? It is exquisite.'

So I tell Leon about Lydia. I tell him everything about her that is exquisite, and everything that makes my heart ache. I've just finished when Balios whinnies and one of the approaching horses returns his greeting. There's a rattling of wheels and we look up to the light of two blazing torches.

Belted with swords and daggers, Danae and Zena descend from their chariots and wedge their torches in the ground. They climb swiftly over the rocks and lean together into the boulder, bracing their feet in the muddy ground. In a few seconds, it starts to move. Danae whispers, 'Slowly, or we'll hurt him more.' Their silhouettes lit by the flickering torches, they strain against the stone; with an infinite slowness, it lifts. Steadying it, they rest it against another huge rock.

Neither Danae nor Zena looks surprised as twenty Krypteians appear out of the dark and Erebos bows in front of Danae. She says with a calm authority, 'We will look after your leader, Erebos. Your task is to find every single one of the cowards who did this to him and deal out summary execution. Apart from the pair that Lycon has already dispatched.'

'With pleasure, my lady.'

As we carry Leon to the chariots on his shield, Danae says, 'Where do you want to go, Lycon?'

'To the forge, my lady. I need to save his upper leg.' I don't add, 'And very likely, his life.' She already knows that.

I will never forget that journey out of the pass and across the battlefield on the plains of Athens. I sat holding Leon close to me on the floor of Zena's chariot, trying to keep him warm, as we rode across those realms of death. I was glad that it was black night, Selene hiding her face from the slaughter that had taken place on that storm-darkened day. I wondered if we would ever see day again after all the killing and the treachery. And I wondered what the fickle gods would make of it all, with my little mistress' comments ringing in my head: "Squabbling children who could throw thunderbolts!" I wondered too what was going to happen with our traitor king.

But right now, all that matters is getting Leon to the forge. Zena has brought water and I hold the flask to his lips. Blood is leaking from his smashed leg onto the floor of the chariot and I worry about how much he has lost. And how badly infection could be setting in, after such a long exposure to that filthy mud. Across these ghostly killing fields, with looters scurrying like jackals over dead and dying Persians, and Spartans and Athenians recovering their fallen comrades' shields and armour before burying their bodies, we ride on through the long night.

Zena and Danae, each in an Achilles chariot, say nothing, except to call to their horses to encourage them as they gallop onwards. If we come across a water trough, they halt to let the animals drink a small amount. Then it's a walk for a mile or so, into a trot for another mile and then a gentle canter before stretching them further. They, as I did on that Persian ride, wish to keep safe the noble animals who serve them so well.

When we reach the forge, it's deserted; Pyro has been fighting, along with many other sixty-year-old Spartans. I fervently hope that my great mentor is in good health. We lay Leon gently on the bench that I used to sleep on and I put a hand on his forehead. He's now dangerously hot; the infection in his lower leg is setting in. I say to Zena, 'We have to get the fire going; I need the heat to make the saw blade clean and safe.' She has the forge fire blasting in no time, while Danae searches for yarrow outside. I say to Leon, 'You know what I have to do, don't you?'

His eyes, bright with fever, go to Danae as she enters with the yarrow. 'What is the news from the field, my lady?'

She kneels next to him and puts a cool hand on his burning forehead. Her voice is firm. 'The Persian King has been killed; Xenophon cut him down. Our men have prevailed; the Persian army is scattering.'

He murmurs, 'Take your time, Wolf Eyes. You and I have no urgent appointments.'

As I start to assemble my instruments, Danae says, 'One moment.' She seats herself on the bench, gently lifts Leon as if he were a child and rests his head in her lap, cradling it in her hands. 'We need to make you as comfortable as possible.'

He whispers, 'I have never been more so. Is it permitted to gaze upon your face, my lady?'

She smiles, like sunlight bursting through clouds. 'I should take it as a grave slight if you did not!'

With a silent prayer to the god Hephaestos, and steady hands, I begin my work. The saw is purified by plunging it into the flames, then Zena cools it outside in the chill air. I tie the leather tourniquet tightly round Leon's thigh. Zena applies the disinfecting yarrow as I open up veins and arteries and tie them off. His poor lower leg, with its splintered bone and festering wounds, is beyond any help save that of the merciful saw. It could be any soldier's leg I am severing with that keen instrument, so detached do I feel about simply doing the very best that I can.

Any time I look up, Leon and Danae are locked in their own private world; if one person's gaze could be intertwined with another's, theirs are. I don't think the gods themselves could glimpse what is passing between Danae and Leon. Nor would these two mortals wish them to.

*

In the dying light of the forge flames, I look at the results of my handiwork. Zena says, 'It's a very clean wound.'

'It should heal well.'

'Shall I give him some water now?'

'Yes. Just small sips.' I reflect with astonishment that this is the first time ever that Zena has asked me what to do. I must be rising still higher in her approval ratings. So I'd better not screw up now. With another silent prayer, this time of thanks to the fire god, I go looking for the materials I need for the next stage of my work. Pyro and I had become much in demand for saving life by sawing off limbs, and we had accumulated a handy store of ash and soft but strong leather. I look for the very best wood and hide, and I think hard about how I can improve the design. Like I did with the chariot.

Leon is mercifully unconscious now, as I gently try my first attempt at his new leg around the stump below his knee, not touching, as the wound will be far too tender, just measuring up. Danae whispers, 'He will be a terrible patient!'

'That's why we have to get him walking again as soon as possible.'

Zena adds, 'And riding. He can do that before he walks. I'll get him on Arion!'

'Zena, you're a genius! That could be just the thing.' She looks at me like I've crowned her with laurels and I find myself going hot with embarrassment. 'I'm going to try another layer of leather, to make it as comfortable as possible.'

Leon's unconsciousness continues until the sun is high in the sky and the air is mild. When he wakes, his skin is a healthy colour and the fever is gone. The pain will be there for a long time, but his life will go on. We give him as much water as he can drink, then it's time to leave. We lift him into Zena's chariot and I sit holding him to my chest. He is exhausted and his head rests on my shoulder. As we clatter away from the forge down Sparta's streets, I remember that I left all our armour, Leon's and mine, scattered on the stone floor, together with my bloodied sword and his. And I think, long may they stay there. It's such a relief to be out of the terrible process of taking life and on the road towards saving it instead.

On the way to Danae's estate, Leon opens his eyes and looks up at the sky. Two eagles are circling again and calling to each other. He murmurs, 'What happens after you've won a war, Wolf Eyes?'

'You get on with peace, while preparing for the next war. You taught me that!'

*

Back at Danae's estate, we learned day by day about the outcome of the war. The allies put paid to the small Persian fleet that was sent to deceive us about the main route of the seaborne invasion. They captured every ship and added it to their own war fleets; the crews were enslaved rather than being needlessly put to the sword.

King Erastus was detained on the night following the battle, as he was preparing to flee. Xenophon's investigations revealed that Erastus had been secretly communicating with the King of Persia for some time. The mercenaries were a force sent by Persia with a view to assassinating Phidias and leaving Erastus as a satrap, or governor, of Persia over Sparta.

A week later, the traitor king was put on trial for his life, a trial that was made very public so that Spartans could see what their surviving king was made of. Erastus protested that he was trying to get the best outcome for Sparta in the face of impossible odds. He claimed that Phidias was an incompetent leader and fell because of his own lack of judgement.

Contradicted by all the evidence against him, this was a patent lie that drew ominous mutterings from those members of the public who were present at the trial. The case against Erastus was further reinforced by Xenophon, who cited the betrayal by Hipparchos and his collusion in the hiring of the mercenary army. This was, very possibly, the worst betrayal of one king by another in the entire history of the Spartan diarchy. At the end of the proceedings, the crowds in the gallery were silent in shock.

In the face of such treachery, the ephors decided not to execute Erastus. That task could fall to someone more appropriate. Instead, they exiled him to Persia, escorted by an armed guard of Krypteian cavalry led by Erebos. Erebos reported back that Erastus went expecting a hero's welcome. Contrary to his expectation, he was beheaded within hours of being received into the court of the new King of Kings.

TEN

BLOOD BROTHERS

Leon was taking his second ride on Arion around the manege when Xenophon arrived on his white charger. As Danae had predicted, Leon was a terrible patient; he demanded far too much of himself, far too soon. So he was trying to canter before he could trot, falling off and cursing himself, and all our patience was wearing out.

But when the master turned up, Leon calmed down. First of all, under Xenophon's quiet instruction, he walked Arion around the manege. Next, with some coaching from the master, he nudged Arion into a sitting trot and we could see his balance improving by the minute. Then Xenophon challenged him to canter, and after the sitting trot this was relatively easy. I'm sure too that Arion had every intention of ensuring that his new and beloved rider would succeed; the canter of an Arabian never seems to touch the earth.

Finally, Leon gave a brilliant demonstration of walking on the wooden leg with the leather harness that I had crafted for him. I had made the shoulder straps broad for comfort and added some bronze figure work for the chest strap that even Pyro said was 'passing good, Wolf Cub'. Leon liked it so much that he asked me if I would do the same decorations for the leather breastplate of his horse's saddle.

On the way to the dining room, I jokingly give him a shove and he staggers then regains his balance, swearing at me. I laugh. 'I couldn't have recovered from that! Remember when I downed you on Mount Taygetos? You had to help me up!'

At last, he laughs. 'I give you that.'

'You gave me far more than that! I could barely walk when you taught me how to fight, how to swim and how to ride a cavalry assault course! Not to mention how to read Homer and Xenophon, and write, and teach geometry!'

'You were a fast learner.'

'So are you – so stop beating yourself up!'

The banter continues until we're sat at the dining table. And there, Xenophon's grave face makes us all go quiet. I notice that Danae and Zena are dressed in beautiful robes that I've never seen before. And they both have gold braids in their hair, which is unusual for Spartan women. Not only that, but Danae said to make sure that we were in our Spartan army crimson for Xenophon's visit. Suddenly, I have the weird feeling that I had all that time ago, when Leon and I dined here after Zena's magnificent chariot race. Only this is like someone else's party entirely.

Xenophon says, 'After Sparta has been left without kings, I have been in lengthy discussion with the ephors. Urgent as well as lengthy because the annual election of the ephors is due next week.' No one speaks. Everyone is looking at this extraordinary statesman, army general, philosopher and historian. I've never worked out what best order to put the titles in.

The master continues, 'Sparta needs kingship and she needs the diarchy; it is the way she has to operate. We have had a problematic past with our last diarchy. But I think, and the ephors agree, that the future augurs well with the two leaders who swept us to victory against the Persians.'

I'm wondering who Xenophon is talking about, when I realise with a shock that it could be Leon and me.

Danae says, 'Two generals have led Sparta into battle with the same unity as two kings joined by blood might have done, is that not so, Xenophon?'

'Indeed it is, my lady. Sparta needs kings like these.'

Danae says to Leon and me, 'Do you know that the Spartan people are calling for you to be their kings?'

Xenophon comments, 'The army, too. On parade, the shout keeps going up.' He adds wryly, 'Anyone would think that we live in a democracy!'

Zena jumps up. 'I'll make sure that the horses are looking their best.'

Xenophon says quietly, 'The ephors and I feel that the wishes of the people and the army must not be denied. So, contrary to everything in this country's tradition, we have arranged a victory parade through the streets of Sparta this afternoon. You may lead as the generals who the people and the army are clamouring to salute. And, if you choose, you may also lead as kings – their dearest wish.'

Leon and I exchange looks. No pressure, then.

*

Laconians are not usually a demonstrative people. I can't recall any other occasion when the streets of Sparta were lined with cheering crowds. The closest is when Zena won that chariot race and drove the spectators wild. On this occasion, Danae and Zena are back in their chariots, driving ahead of us and looking like warrior goddesses with their gold-adorned hair and flowing robes.

Riding side by side with Leon, I feel hot with embarrassment, but looking at him, I see a slight smile on his face. He's riding Arion with way more confidence now, and the black Arabian is stepping out proudly with his dancing walk. I joke, 'Race you?' and he laughs like the old Leon. I'm riding Circe, who is doing her best to steal the show from Arion.

Suddenly, a girl who looks around twelve or thirteen breaks from the crowd and approaches Leon, carrying a bunch of wild thyme. The procession halts to let her hand it to him and he takes it with a gracious bow. With a dainty curtsey, she melts back into the crowd, but her gesture is the signal for everyone thronging the streets of Sparta to start throwing flowers at us. Which simply deepens my embarrassment. Leon notices and laughs again: 'You'd better get used to it, Wolf Eyes. They obviously like your pretty face!' And at last I can see the funny side of it.

When we get to the barracks, the infantry and cavalry, under the command of Xenophon, are lined up with their bronze armour flashing in the sun. And I find this an emotional moment: being welcomed so warmly by men who have followed us so bravely through everything. Looking at Leon's very bright blue eyes, I can see he's feeling the same.

*

The morning after the procession, Leon asked Danae if she would do him the great honour of becoming his wife. He told me afterwards that she said she had loved him from the day she first met him, when he came to ask her if she would take on Zena as her protégé. Something I suspected when I saw the way she looked at him at Zena's victory dinner, and every other time when I saw them together.

I knew that I had to wait until Zena was twenty before I could venture the big question, and that was some months away. But there was another question in my mind that I also badly needed to get an answer to, if answer there was. I knew what I wanted the answer to be, and I was dreading that it might not be what I wanted. But I had to ask, all the same. I began by talking to Leon one day when we were riding out together. As usual, I had trouble trying to work out how to begin, and as usual, he sensed it. 'Out with it, Wolf Eyes.'

'The first and the second night when you caught Zena and me on the mountain… you thought she was my sister?'

'Ah…' He looks ahead of him and then back to me. 'I'm afraid my motives were less than honourable, Wolf Eyes. I was seeking a denial from you, or from her.'

'You wanted her not to be my sister?'

'I was seeking clarification.'

'Because that's the way the Krypteia operates?'

'Partly, yes. But I'm afraid that my motives were selfish as well.'

'You fell in love with her, didn't you?'

'Who would not have done?'

'And then you got your denial…'

He laughs. 'And very shortly after, got thrown! No, I could see a closeness between you that, if it was not between brother and sister, had to be that of a young man and woman who loved each other. That told me to back off.'

'And shortly after that, you met the woman who was to become your wife.'

He looks at me, remembering, as the horses set a gentle walking rhythm. 'To fall in love once was a dizzying experience. But the second time, I thought I would never stop falling.'

'Will you tell me about when you first met your future wife?'

'With the greatest pleasure. But first I must tell you something that is painful to recount. It had made me take great care to avoid ever being seen by Danae, because of the grief this could cause her.'

'Is this to do with the death of her husband?'

He says, even more quietly than usual, 'Yes, Wolf Eyes. Because the man who betrayed Danae's husband to his death was my father.'

Words fail me at that point. The horses carry on walking gently. All I can do is wait for Leon to resume. 'I only found out some time afterwards. I was away from home, living with the other students in the university. My teachers must have known. And it would have been very easy for them to have ostracised me, tainted by my father's guilt. But they did not. Rather, I think, they protected me. And urged me to be the very best that I could, in order to graduate into the Krypteia. Once there, it was easy to ensure that Danae's paths and mine would never cross.'

'Until you met Zena.'

'Until I met you and Zena. At first, I wrote to Danae about Zena, to spare her the sight and sound of me. She wrote back, saying she would consider my request only if I went to see her in person.'

'She would never have blamed the son for the crimes of the father.'

'It would have been perfectly understandable if she had.'

'And so, there you are, feeling more nervous than ever in your life.'

'Terrified is the better word.'

'But you had nothing to fear, did you?'

'She revealed herself to me instantly as a woman of outstanding integrity as well as astounding beauty.' Leon tells me how Danae's first concern when he asked her if she would take on Zena was Myra and Milos. How would these poor farmers manage, having already lost me, if they were also to lose Zena?

Leon says, looking shame-faced, 'I had never even considered this when I claimed you for the Krypteia. But Danae insisted on bringing with her two of her young grooms when we went to see Milos and Myra. She said it would do the grooms good to work on a farm, and she would contribute to their upkeep. She was as good as her word.'

'And that changed the way you did your recruiting?'

'I could see at once – at last! – that if the men I took for the army were needed at home, then replacements had to be provided or livelihoods would be lost.'

I can't help smiling. 'So you were under the influence of a very good woman long before you asked her to marry you.'

Leon brings Arion to a halt and Circe stops too. He looks at me closely. 'You still have something to ask me, Wolf Eyes.'

'Yes. Do Zena and I look like we could be brother and sister?'

'You both have dark hair. You have amber eyes, she has brown, but siblings often have different-coloured eyes. You are of similar build; both of you very strong.'

'So it's a yes.'

'It's a maybe.' He nudges Arion expertly from a standstill to a canter. 'Come on!'

Half an hour later, we're outside Milos and Myra's cottage. The sheep are in the upper pastures at this time of year, and Milos is up there with his two young shepherds. But Myra welcomes us warmly, giving us both a hug that brings tears to my eyes. In her motherly way, she insists on sitting us down with some figs and watered wine. And suddenly, all the time I've been away from here feels like a vivid dream.

Myra asks about Zena and tells us that she and Danae visit quite often, which makes me the shame-faced one now. I resolve to change this. Then, with the conversation over, Myra is looking at me with a kindly smile, and once again, I am tongue-tied. Leon comes to my rescue. 'I will speak for my friend, honourable lady, because this is difficult for him. To speak plainly, he dearly wishes to marry Zena when she comes of age. Only, he is concerned that he and she might be brother and sister. He wonders if you might be able to enlighten him.'

Myra looks at me and her eyes are glistening with tears; my heart is about to break, when she says, 'Milos and I had always hoped you two might marry.'

'So… we're not siblings?'

'No, my dear. You see, when we found you, I guessed who your mother was. You looked so like her, with your beautiful little face. We were friends as girls, and I knew she would never have wanted you to be abandoned. I went to her the next day, to tell her that you had been saved. She and her husband had been told by the city elders that you must not be allowed to live, so we had to keep it all secret.'

Again I'm struggling to speak, thinking of all the grief that came with my birth and near-death. So it's Leon who says gently, 'And Zena…?'

'Alas, my dear, I don't know who her parents were. But we found her as a full-term, newly born babe only four months after finding Lycon – so she could not possibly be his sister.'

We're nearly back at Danae's estate, when I summon the courage to ask, 'What became of your father, Leon?'

'As soon as the army returned from the campaign, he was called to account. Put on trial, condemned and executed that night.'

'It must have been terrible for your mother.'

'I am convinced it was the shame that drove her to an early grave. If only she could have lived long enough to see the happiness that Danae and I enjoy now. It would have helped to heal her poor soul.'

It must have been this tragedy that drove Leon to strive to avert a second one. One day, he rides with me and Zena to pay Milos and Myra one of our now-regular visits; there, waiting for us outside the cottage with Myra, is a very beautiful, dark-haired woman. As I swing off my horse, her eyes look straight into mine with such immediate recognition that I move to her swiftly and take her in my arms. She looks from me to Zena and whispers, 'My dearest son, I could not be more happy for you.' My mother tells me that she recognised me in the victory parade and threw me flowers. Soon after this reunion, my father having died several years before, she comes to live with Myra and Milos.

*

Three months later, we're sat, Danae, Leon and I, in the front row of the chariot race finals of the Olympic Games. This time, Zena has a truly god-given team. Circe on the inside to dance them all around the course, with Arion flying on the outside, the mighty Balios and Xanthos holding firm and fleet in the middle.

The Achilles chariot had already caused quite a stir in the heats because of its phenomenal strength and big wheels. There had been complaints from losing competitors that it was an unfair design. To which the judges responded that the entire purpose of the Olympic Games was to improve fighting excellence, something that the Achilles chariot had been proven beyond doubt to do in the latest war. The opposition was silenced.

So now, there is Zena on the start line, calm in the chariot I made for her. And I'm feeling as nervous as I was the first time I saw her race. Next to me, Leon says teasingly, 'Can't look, Wolf Eyes?'

'It's alright for you. Your wife won't be riding or driving horses for a while now.' Danae is in the first months of pregnancy and looking radiant. She laughs. 'I'm afraid Leon caught me working Circe on the lunge rein just yesterday; I felt she wasn't co-operating fully with the rest of the team.'

'Since when did mares co-operate, my lady?'

'Oh, I think she took my lesson to heart, Lycon. Like all Arabians, she really wants to please.'

Suddenly they're off. And Zena's team is exploding into the lead. I have never seen a vehicle move so fast. Leon and I sit holding our breath as the Achilles chariot soars ahead, its strength battle-tested to the ultimate. My heart goes out to those noble horses whom I know so well: Balios and Xanthos, Arion and Circe. Who are powering around the circuit with Zena calling them on to victory. Twelve circuits that seem to go on for ever. Sometimes I still see them in slow motion, the horses dancing to the melody of Lydia's beautiful song. Zena is so far ahead that it's a triumph ride all the way. And this time, the chariot is in one piece as they thunder across the finishing line. As Zena waves to the ecstatic crowds and we stand to applaud her, Leon looks at me. 'The woman you love turns twenty today, doesn't she, Wolf Eyes?'

'Do you think she'll accept me?'
'She did that long ago.'

*

Kings and their queens need a job of work to do, so a great deal went on as usual after Leon and I were crowned Sparta's kings and Zena and I were married. Six months after the Olympic Games, he became the proud father of twin boys, after a long and difficult labour for Danae. But as she said herself, there is absolutely nothing easy about producing one child, let alone two of them in one go. Visibly relieved that mother and babies were in the best of health, Leon was firmly told to get on with his job and let Danae get on with hers.

He was determined to continue recruiting, because Sparta's army still needed building with fearless helots who became good soldiers; in turn they were rewarded with their own land and freedom. Xenophon keenly supported us in this, the beginning of great change in the ways of Sparta and Spartan law. Very gradually, we were beginning to move from being a predominantly slave society towards one of freemen. Leon and I also continued the annual games that had been set up under the previous kings. It gave our soldiers the chance to be recognised for and celebrate their prowess, and Sparta's citizens the chance to applaud them.

Danae and Zena carried on training the charioteers and supplying the cavalry with top-quality animals. Then came one day when Danae showed us a new arrival at her estate who, she said, was not going to become just anyone's cavalry horse. Leon and I watch Zena lead the jet-black Arabian foal on his first outing around the manege. He has the beginnings of the same dancing walk of his father, on the wobbliest of long gangly legs. Circe looks on proudly, as Danae gently strokes her golden neck. 'Our sons will learn to ride on lesser animals and earn this boy as their reward, when he's old enough.'

I can't take my eyes off the little Arion. 'What will you call him, my lady?'

'The way his father flies… it has to be Pegasus, doesn't it, Lycon?'

A few days later, I get a letter from Philemon:

My dear Lycon,

Please accept my heartfelt congratulations on your elevation to joint kingship of Sparta with Leon; I am sure that you will lead your people as nobly in peacetime as you did in the war.

Liddy was married to my good friend Aristides a week ago. I know that her lessons with you will help her to take up the reins of managing a household with great confidence.

Your friend,
Philemon of Athens

Zena looks up from her reading in surprise as I shamble round the room. 'This can't be right! Married to a man who is nearly as old as her father!'

'Is this your little pupil?'

'Zena, I am so frightened for Lydia. She is barely fourteen years old!'

She murmurs, 'The poor child. To be married so terribly young. And to such an old man. Just because that's the way they do things in Athens doesn't mean it's good for her!'

That night, I dream of Lydia on her flying horse. I hear her crystal voice and singing lyre. She's traversing cloud kingdoms, and she looks as excited as when I told her about Balios. Then I wake in Zena's arms, my eyes full of tears. She strokes my face and I embrace her like I never want to let her go.

*

One year onwards, Zena and I are still without children. And without any words being said, it starts to hurt both of us, each of us wondering if it's our fault. Without any bidding, the same fear strikes each of us – is that why we were dumped on Mount Taygetos? Are we rubbish after all? This is the cruellest thing possible, which I never imagined could happen. But irrational or not, this is what we both can't help thinking. Leon is aware of it too. But he has no idea what to say, with his bouncing twin sons. How could he know? What could he say?

Time drags on and Zena and I are still struggling, hanging on together, in the desert of childlessness. Then, I get another letter from Philemon and I dread opening it, so certain am I of its contents:

My dear Lycon,

It is with a breaking heart that I write to tell you of the death of our beloved Lydia. Married to Aristides for just over a year, she was rejoicing with her husband over

the imminent arrival of their first child. Alas, the labour
was a long and cruel one. The child, a girl, was born dead.
My darling daughter lived for just another day and night,
before being carried away by a terrible fever. To my great
sadness, I was unable even to reach her in time to say our
last farewells.

My wife and I miss Liddy dreadfully, and always will.
Among our consolations is the happy time she spent with
you as her tutor. I salute you and Leon on the thrones of
Sparta; your little pupil would be very proud of you, as
am I.

I feel strongly that our two countries have much
to learn from each other. We have joined hands in this
terrible battle against our common foe. Let us stay firm
so that war may never again threaten so much of what is
precious to us.

Your friend,
Philemon of Athens

I show the letter to Zena. We both feel so close to the
edge that nothing other than a night walk up a mountain
together can prevent a descent into utter despair. So we set
off like we used to on our climbs up Mount Taygetos, when
we were teenagers watching sheep.

On the way up, we notice the ledge where we saw the
magnificent wolf crowned with Selene's silver. Over the
ridge, and we're looking down on the place where Zena
fought off the men who would kill our sheep. And now,
twenty feet above us like ghosts rise the Krypteia, with Leon
at their head. Something in his eyes tells me that he knows

everything. He says in his quiet voice, 'I was coming for you. Follow me, Wolf Eyes.'

And so, once again, I follow Leon. He takes us upwards on a steep climb. We can feel the temperature dropping as we rise. Then we see the light of a fire. But this is no helot rebellion. More Krypteian soldiers are camped around the flames. In the glow, one of them is tenderly holding a swaddled baby; it's crying in a weak voice. Gently, the soldier hands the child into Zena's waiting arms. Torches blaze in the night as Leon and I walk either side of Zena back down the mountain, his men following, to Danae's estate, where food and life await this tiny soul.

Our beloved daughter is named Lydia. Leon says she rides Pegasus better than either of his sons.